A Slice of
Bakewell Tart

DEDICATION

In loving memory of mum and dad.

ACKNOWLEDGMENTS

After a lifetime of writing non-fiction, this book was a personal challenge.

I have thoroughly enjoyed the creative process of developing the story and bringing the characters to life.

I have been encouraged and helped throughout the journey by many people, including my mum, who sadly is no longer here to witness its publication. I will be eternally grateful to her for developing my passion for writing and for her support.

Thanks also to my loving husband Tony for his patience, cheerleading and endless cups of tea!

I would also like to acknowledge the help and support of my beta readers and a special thank you to Jenny Kartupelis and Lynnda Worsnop.

.

Chapter One

Tom walked down the garden path and closed the gate behind him. He paused to button up his coat against the cool morning air, and then he strode off towards town. Turning the corner, he noticed a small brown knitted toy on the pavement in front of him. A dinosaur. He picked it up and called out to the young woman ahead of him.

"Excuse me. I think you have dropped something."

She turned to see where the voice was coming from. Quickening his pace to catch up with her, he noticed the young boy in the pushchair. He had a mop of blond hair and bright blue eyes. Tom stooped to his eye level and offered him the dinosaur, making it dance as it moved closer to the boy's outstretched hand. The child giggled in appreciation and clutched the toy tightly.

"Thank you," said the young woman. "It would have been tears for the rest of the day if he had lost that. He is mad for dinosaurs."

"Not a problem. He is a cutie." Tom said, nodding towards the young boy. The woman smiled and headed off down the road. Tom continued his short walk to the cafe. The tiny fingers of the boy's hands were imprinted on his mind. He couldn't recall a time when his own children's hands had been quite as small.

"Afternoon, Tom. Your usual?"

"Yes, please, Alice. Not so nice out there."

Tom wasn't used to having 'a usual.' He wasn't accustomed to building up such familiarity. He had only been coming to the cafe for the last couple of months since his wife's illness had got too much that he needed a break, but it seemed that qualified him as a regular. The cafe wasn't a fancy place, but it was welcoming. Photographs and paintings of local views adorned the pale walls, and a mismatch of vintage tea cups and saucers balanced precariously on pine shelves. The harsh strip lighting let the place down and cast unwelcome shadows across the tables, each bearing a small glass jar with a stem of fresh flowers.

Alice - she had introduced herself on his second visit - was a pretty young thing. He guessed she was in her late twenties. She wore her dark hair in a ponytail and had a penchant for vest tops that revealed her bra straps which Tom thought made her look rather untidy. He thought of his daughter and the arguments throughout her teenage years about having too much on show when she went out. Alice had plenty to say, regaling each customer with conversation. She had the full range from the weather to politics, depending on how long it took to serve you. Tom was quite taken with her, and she certainly made coming to the cafe all the more enjoyable.

He picked up the plate and mug of tea from the

counter and made his way to the corner table. The steamy windows didn't allow much of a view, but he liked the idea of being next to the hustle and bustle of the high street.

After loosening his raincoat, he eased himself into the seat and sighed. Taking his first sip of tea, he could feel his shoulders drop, and the tension in his neck start to soften. Wednesday again, he thought, halfway through another week. And what did he have to look forward to this week? The highlights would be collecting his pension, fish and chips on Friday and a trip to the library van. It wasn't much, but Tom took comfort from the routine. A certain regularity of people and places brought reassurance. A sense of not being alone in the world. A connection, however tenuous, to the people sharing the same spaces. Getting used to his own company was a new experience. When the Navy posted him abroad, he knew what homesickness felt like and missed his wife and family, but he would never let himself be alone long enough to wallow. He had always sought out company, whether that of his fellow shipmates or even the company of strangers. He always needed to feel close to another human being, even if that meant sharing the same air as them in a dark and dingy bar in some far-flung corner of the Far East.

Having had a good circle of family and friends previously, he found his world had become very small and increasingly oppressive. His parents and siblings were long gone, and friends were spread literally around the world. Having lived in the town most of his life, Tom was on nodding terms with most people he passed in the street, but for the most part, he had spent his retirement in the company of his wife, the kids and the grandkids. They were usually enough to sustain him. Thankfully his son and daughter and the grandchildren all lived within an hour's drive, so at least he could see them regularly. He had a chance to experience with the grandchildren the things he had missed out on when his own two were little, and he was away at sea, and for that, he was very grateful. Up until very recently, if anyone had asked him, he would have said he was happy. Now, he felt a shadow across his world. He worried about his children. Brian was having some problems, although Tom didn't know the nature of them. Julie was lonely - not that she had said as much, but Tom often thought it noticeable in her eyes; but more than anything, he was terrified of losing his beloved Brenda.

What he felt today was a whole new set of emotions that had crept into his world like an invasive weed, clouding his memories and strangling his thoughts of future happiness. The feeling was inextricably linked to his wife's decline. The more dementia took hold of Brenda, the more this new, haunting feeling of unease grabbed at Tom's very soul.

As he drank his tea and bit into his first mouthful of Bakewell Tart, he took a moment to savour the sweet icing and the first taste of almond. He had always liked Bakewell Tart, even as a young lad. He closed his eyes as he took his second bite and was immediately transported to the kitchen of his childhood with wonderful aromas of freshly baked treats. His mother smudged with icing sugar, looking harassed and content in equal measure. It wasn't a large room, but it was the epicentre of his childhood. It was a homely kitchen, with rather too much furniture in the small space. A sizeable Welsh dresser filled one wall stacked with his mother's favourite blue and white striped pottery. Everything happened there; family meals, endless loads of laundry, emergency surgery on his sister's dolls. There was always a pot of something boiling away on the stove, and there was always a hug on offer if life wasn't treating you well. He could do with a hug now, he thought.

Chapter Two

Liz clicked off the television and stood up, time for a cup of tea. As she straightened her back, a slight grimace crossed her face as her muscles spasmed and locked back in place. Getting old was nothing to smile about. She shuffled to the kitchen and flicked the switch on the kettle. As she opened the fridge door, she saw with disappointment the empty bottle of milk. How had she managed to run out again? It only seemed two minutes since she bought that pint of milk.

Checking she had some change, she pulled on her coat and headed out for the high street. The rain made her blink as she made her way down to the local shops.

As she turned the corner, she saw the lights coming from the Willow Tree Coffee House. Liz couldn't remember the last time she had ventured into a café alone. She was used to doing things as part of a couple or with the family. Being a widow was still something she was getting used to, and she hadn't yet embraced the idea of having days out unless accompanied by her daughter or friend. She had never enjoyed her own company, and even after the best part of a year, she was still getting used to the idea of being a party of one.

She took a deep breath, turned the door handle and headed inside. The warmth of the air thick with the aroma of coffee made her catch her breath. "A cup of tea, please," she said to the young girl behind the counter and then seeing a tempting row of cakes and pastries behind the glass shelf ", and a piece of Bakewell Tart."

As she turned to find a seat, she noticed the lone man by the window. He had short salt and pepper hair and was wearing a smart brown jumper. Had he felt her eyes burning into the back of his neck? For whatever reason, he turned round and almost instantly seemed to know her face. He smiled warmly, which created pleats of crow's feet around his eyes.

"Tom, is it you?" She ventured.

"Sit down before you fall. You look like you have seen a ghost. Am I such a sight?"

"I can't believe it's you, and I can't believe that you recognised me after all these years."

"Painful, is it?" Tom asked, noticing the discomfort that registered on Liz's face as she slid herself into the wooden bench.

"Aye, a touch of arthritis," she said.

Tom gave her a few minutes to regain her composure and then continued:

"What brings you to these parts, Liz? Don't tell me we have been living within spitting distance all these years and never knew?"

That would be too much to bear.

Tom had played out this scene a million times what he would say if he ever came face to face with Liz Hargreaves. His first love. The girl that had broken his heart and driven him as far away from home as he could get. Of course, no one knew of his musings over the decades, as he had pictured her as the dutiful wife and mother. Whenever he went to a new place, he would secretly cast around, wondering if she was one of the faces in the crowd.

Marriage should have stopped his interest in other women, but it had never stopped him from looking. Now here they were, sitting in a down-at-heel seaside cafe reminiscing over tea and Bakewell Tart. It was nothing like he imagined, but it was real, and it was happening right now. His rehearsed speech was redundant. He had a million questions, thoughts were racing through his head, but there was no time now. He marvelled at her beauty. Her eyes were as vivid as ever, Siamese blue, just like he remembered. Her face, so familiar yet etched now with the ups and downs that life had thrown at her. He wanted to lean over and kiss her, but he knew that wasn't appropriate.

He felt there should be more to mark the occasion, perhaps a fanfare. He didn't want it to end, but he was conscious that it was nearly 2.30 pm. He didn't have long, and soon he would have to walk away. He had just found Liz after 50 years. How could he leave? He had to find a way of seeing her again.

"Don't worry. I have just moved here within the last few months. After my husband died, I didn't want to be rattling around the house alone, so I decided to move nearer to my daughter. I've always liked it here and fancied living at the seaside. I've got one of the new bungalows up on the ridge. I get a great sea view, and it's near enough for me to walk to the shops. I was on my way there now to buy a pint of milk when I felt drawn to come in here."

"Must have been my magnetism", joked Tom. "Do you remember the last time we were here together? We came on a day trip with the youth club. Those were the days."

"I do remember, quite vividly. We had a good time. Have you lived here long?

"Most of my married life. After you, you know left" - did that make him sound bitter? - "I joined the Navy. A couple of years later, I married, and we set up round here. I retired a few years back. The kids live reasonably close, and I've three grandkids now, so it's worked out OK. And you?"

"Yes, I suppose I've done alright. Had a good life – not always easy, but then I don't imagine any of us have it easy."

"So what happened to you? The last time we saw each other, you were catching a bus to London to study to be a midwife. Is that what you became?"

"Not exactly. I decided midwifery wasn't for me. I came back North, we used to live just outside Grangestone, and I worked in the local hospital. I have always felt more comfortable looking after working-class folk than the types I met in London. It was in The General where I met Frank."

"Frank? Was he one of the doctors?"

"No", Liz replied, amused. She had had her fair

share of admirers, and she could tell some tales about the antics of some doctors and consultants, but those stories were not for general consumption. She had learned over the years that some things were best kept private.

"Nothing of the sort, Frank was a miner. He had cut his finger badly and needed stitches. It was very romantic. Him with his finger end hanging off and me doing my Florence Nightingale bit."

"I can imagine!" Tom smiled. "Love at first sight!"

"I wouldn't go that far, but we had a nice chat, and he seemed a good sort. We made arrangements to meet on my next day off, and that was it. Six months later, we were married. What about you? And what about your wife?" Liz prompted.

"Brenda. We have had a good marriage. We couldn't have children, so we adopted two, a boy, Brian and a girl, Julie. Brenda has dementia. It started a few months ago, and it is taking its toll. Some days she hardly knows me. I don't usually leave her, but Brian comes round on a Wednesday and stays with her while I pop out. I either come here for a change of scenery or run a few errands. The kids have been very supportive, but they have their own lives."

"It must be hard for you, Tom." Liz stirred her tea absentmindedly and took a drink. Losing Frank had been tough, but it had been sudden. She had no time to prepare for it, and whilst there was no chance to say goodbye, there had been no long illness to endure. For a moment, Liz tried to imagine what it would have been like seeing Frank deteriorate before her eyes. In that instant, she decided that the car crash, whilst brutal, was perhaps the easier option.

"Yes, I can't pretend otherwise. I try my best, but there are some days when I wonder if I can go on. Some days Brenda doesn't even know who I am. Sorry, I don't mean to drag the conversation down."

Conversation flowed easily between the two for the next hour, but things had to come to an end all too soon. As much as Tom wanted to spend the rest of the day talking to Liz, he knew he had to get back home. It wasn't fair to keep Brian waiting.

"Liz, I am sorry to do this, but I do have to go. Is there any chance we could continue this conversation next Wednesday?"

"That would be lovely, Tom. We have barely scratched the surface. I could do with a friend, and I haven't had a chance to meet anyone as yet apart from my neighbours."

"I'll see you at the same time next week then." and with that, Tom was out of the door.

Chapter Three

Leaving the café, Tom made his way back home. It was only a short walk, but it felt like a significant achievement. Not because he was unfit or infirm, quite the opposite, he took pride in his health and keeping in good shape. He was still reeling from the unexpected encounter. Who pops out for an hour and finds themselves face to face with someone who had been such a significant part of their life 50 years ago?

As he turned the key in the lock, he took a deep breath and fixed his face to a smile.

"I'm back", he called out as he entered the hallway and hung his coat on the polished hook.

"You were gone longer than you said," said Brian, emerging from the kitchen.

"Yes, sorry about that, I got talking to someone I haven't seen in years. It was nice to chat."

"Old flame, was it?" Brian teased. His son had a way of making the most innocuous of situations sound sordid. He would have made a fortune writing the double entendres for seaside postcards, thought Tom, smiling wryly.

"Something like that." Tom couldn't be bothered to enter into a discussion. The few minutes he had spent with Liz had been somewhat monumental, and he wanted to enjoy them in private. Later, he would go over every word and relive the time they had spent this afternoon and their time together in their youth. To share the experience with Brian would be to taint it and open it up for examination and unwanted scrutiny. No, the details were for him to know and him alone.

"Anyway, how are things here? How's your mum?"

"Usual. No change. We had a cup of tea and a flick through the photo album. Mum loves that. The best thing we ever did was put all the family photos together in one place."

It was such a simple idea, and Brian was right. Having the photos to look at had reignited a spark in Brenda. She might not always remember what day it was, but show her a picture of the kids like toddlers or their wedding, and she could recall every detail. It was these precious moments that Tom cherished. They were fleeting and becoming more so with every passing week but a few minutes reminiscing together was pure gold. It reminded Tom of the good times and helped him cope with the bad.

"Anyway, dad, it's time I was going. Cheryl's cooking tonight, and I have to pick the kids up on the way home." Brian was edging towards the door. "Same time next week?"

"Yes, please, son and thanks again."

It had taken some doing to establish this weekly routine of Tom getting some respite from his caring duties, but Tom couldn't begin to explain how much it meant to him. God knows he loved his wife, and he was a devoted husband, father, grandfather and carer, but the hours together took their toll on his wellbeing, and those precious few minutes away from the house were sheer bliss. A change of scenery, time to regroup and permission to think about himself or at least not think about his wife for a while.

Of course, he hadn't asked for help, certainly not in the beginning. How could he? He was her husband. He had sworn his vows, in sickness and in health, till death do us part. So it was his duty to take care of Brenda, just like she had looked after the four of them all her life, and in the first few weeks, he had coped. He made cups of tea, he was no stranger to the kitchen and could produce a tasty meal, and he helped her up and down from her chair.

Her decline had been much quicker than anticipated, though, and recently things had taken a turn for the worse. When alone in bed at night, Tom often wondered how it had come to this. It was only a matter of months since they went to see Mr Ramadi, the consultant.

They had gone as a family to the appointment. Funny, if you had suggested getting together to go out for dinner, it would have taken weeks of planning and endless checking of diaries and email. What with the grand children's numerous after-school activities and Brian and Julie's busy work schedules, but suddenly it was no problem when it came to going to the hospital appointment.

I suppose I should be grateful for that, thought Tom, and of course he was. He appreciated the moral support, but it still made him smile. Not that going to the hospital was on par with eating out at a restaurant; he wasn't trying to make light of the situation; no, it was just that it showed, if they wanted to do something, like be together, they could be. Family dinners obviously didn't rank very highly on their list of priorities.

It had been a dark, wet, miserable day when they went to the hospital. Brenda was looking smart in a mauve skirt and navy cardigan. Oblivious to what was about to unfold, if she thought anything, then it was that she was going to town for a spot of shopping, and why shouldn't she believe that? Ordinarily, that is what they would have been doing on a Friday morning. Regular as clockwork. That had been their routine. Drive to town, have a look in the Coop and then fish and chips in Harvey's before coming home.

Brian had driven them in his car to take the stress off Tom, and with four of them on board, it was more comfortable than shoehorning into Tom's tiny vehicle. The journey had been fraught.

Brian wasn't the best of drivers, and he tended to blame everyone else on the road for his shortcomings. Before long, the air was blue as Brian called the other imbeciles on the road all the names under the sun. So much for taking the stress away, thought Tom.

When they arrived at the hospital, finding

somewhere to park had been the next challenge. In the end, getting perilously close to the time of their appointment, Brian had dropped them off outside reception and, having parked in the furthest corner of the hospital grounds, walked back to join them. He found the three of them, motionless sitting in the waiting room, staring up at the screen, willing it to display Brenda's name as the next patient.

A further twenty minutes passed in near silence as they sat, expectantly. Tom couldn't help noticing the incredible amount of posters that greeted his eye. Questions and challenges bombarded his senses from every direction:

'Are you clear on cancer?'

'Did you know missed appointments last year cost the NHS £11million.. .'

Breastfeeding, emergency exits, glaucoma, and totals raised in charity fundraising were all there jostling for attention. How could anyone take in this much information? For him, it was overwhelming. Tom wished the walls were blank so he could be alone with his thoughts. And there was a radio. As if the posters and the electronic screen were not enough. A radio, tuned to some Godforsaken local radio station, was blaring out endless, mindless drivel interspersed with tuneless music and irritating adverts for MOTs and Six Form Colleges. It was too much to bear.

Finally, Brenda's name appeared in bright blue letters on the screen. Slowly they got to their feet and made their way into the consultant's room. Mr

Ramadi smiled as he welcomed them in, and they got settled into position. He was a tall, elegant man with a gentle voice and a soothing bedside manner.

"I have the results of the tests," he said, cutting straight to the chase, a trait Tom greatly appreciated. He couldn't bear suspense, and it seemed the modern way to keep people waiting for the answer. All those endless quizzes and so-called talent shows had created a trend for building tension. "It is, as I suspected, Alzheimer's," he continued.

After that, Tom wasn't sure he heard anything else. They didn't leave the room for almost half an hour, but Tom was absent for 29 of those minutes. That was where the kids came in. Each of them picked up on different parts of the conversation. Brian, the sensitive one, was more concerned with his mum and what she was experiencing, whilst Julie, the practical one, focused on what she would need in terms of short and long term care arrangements.

And as for Brenda? She had no idea what was going on. For the most part, she sat quietly, letting the others talk around her. Occasionally she would ask if it was time to go and was it today she had fish and chips.

"I know this is a huge challenge for all of you", Mr Ramadi was saying when Tom finally tuned back into the conversation in the room. "It is essential to be as honest as you can with Brenda.

"Try not to belittle what she is saying or have an

argument. Her ability to understand and make sense of the world will change over time, and how quickly that happens is hard to say. For now, remember, she is still your wife, Tom and your mother, Brian, Julie. Make the most of each precious day and build your memories for the future."

In the spirit of keeping things regular, the four of them decamped from the hospital to Harvey's for the weekly treat; only today, Brenda was the only one with any appetite.

The first few days after the diagnosis had passed in a bit of a blur. Everyone was upset. Tom had known something was wrong and had suspected dementia, but there was something about hearing the words from a specialist that made the situation more serious, more permanent.

"So that's that then", he had said as they made their way from the consulting room back to the car.

"Don't worry, dad, we are here to help", said Julie, trying to put on a brave face. She meant well, but Tom knew that as a single parent with a five-year-old to look after, she didn't have much time to dedicate to looking after him or Brenda.

As for Brian, he had a busy job, two youngsters making demands on his time and a wife who wasn't that keen on spending time with the 'old folk'.

"Thanks, love, that's kind, but I'll manage." He had meant it as well. That's what you did, managed. He was a practical man who could turn his hand to most things. He had been a good husband and a doting father. He might not have been around to read bedtime stories, but if you needed something mending, whether it was a washing machine, a climbing frame or the family car, he would have it sorted in no time.

They had settled into a good routine. Tom would help Brenda wash and dress, and then they would have breakfast in the dining room before sitting down to daytime television. Tom would see to the housework and bring fresh cups of tea at regular intervals. The conversation was hit and miss. Some days Brenda was as lucid as she had ever been, and they would chat merrily as if nothing was wrong. Occasionally she would forget a particular word or where she was going with her train of thought, the thing that had initially triggered concerns in Tom. Other days, she hardly recognised Tom and refused to speak. Those were the hardest to bear.

Brenda had always been a word smith, enjoying crosswords and any form of word games, Scrabble being a particular favourite. When she started to forget words and mix up her sentences, Tom instinctively knew something was amiss. He had made a doctor's appointment, and in weeks, she had an appointment with the specialist.

What he hadn't bargained for was the emotional strain the following months would put on him. Cooking and cleaning, he took in his stride, even getting used to the more delicate issues like taking

Brenda to the toilet and getting her bathed he handled. What got him down was the coldness in her eyes. The way she looked right through him rather than at him. Where once there was a sparkle, now there was glassiness.

It had been about three months after that fateful day in Mr Ramadi's office that Brian had found his dad sobbing. Brian had popped round to see how things were when he discovered his father hunched over the sink in the kitchen. He had never seen his father cry.

Tom was a loving father, but he wasn't one for showing his feelings. As a family, they laughed and joked, and there could be stern words if the children had done something to annoy him, but he didn't display many emotions.

"It's nothing, just ignore me", Tom had said when he was conscious that Brian had entered the kitchen.

"It's OK, dad. I understand, and you don't have to pretend with me. Tell me what's wrong and how I can help."

They had moved to sit at the kitchen table, and Tom wiped his tired eyes.

"I knew it was going to be tough, but it breaks my heart when she doesn't know who I am. Some days, I have difficulty getting her to eat something as she is so suspicious of me. I just want your mum back."

"I know, dad. You are doing brilliantly. I'd do more myself, but it's hard to find the time with the job and the kids. What can I do?"

Over coffee, they had hatched the plan for Brian to come and sit with his mother once a week on a Wednesday. Tom wasn't sure how Brian squared it with his employer, but he didn't ask. It wasn't much respite in a week, but it had made all the difference.

When Brian had gone and Brenda was happily watching television, Tom stretched out on the sofa and started to replay the events of the morning. Being reunited with Liz had been a wonderful surprise. He wasn't quite sure what he was getting himself into, but he couldn't wait to see her again.

Chapter Four

It had been such an unexpected turn of events –
popping out for a pint of milk and ending up in a
café and meeting up with someone she hadn't seen
for the best part of a lifetime that Liz didn't know
what to do next.

She felt stimulated, too hyper to go home and flop
down in front of the television. Instead, she
decided she would take an amble along the sea
front and pick up the much-needed pint of milk
from the shop on the corner.

The rain had stopped, and weak sunshine pushed
through the grey clouds making the idea of a stroll
more inviting. May and the town was already
starting to bustle again with day-trippers and early
holiday makers. Liz had always loved the sea, and
coming to live at the seaside had been a lifelong
ambition only realised after Frank had died. Her
daughter had persuaded her to move.

Liz was sad that Frank hadn't been able to join
her on this part of their journey. He, too, loved the
sea, in fact, any water. He liked to fish and would
spend days sitting in quiet contemplation by a river
bank, something Liz could never do. She was too
fidgety. They had tried it once, going together. She
recalled how she had packed a picnic and thought
it would be a lovely way to spend time together in
the countryside. The reality, well, the boredom,
had hit her after about an hour of trying to sit

quietly. Even though she had taken a book, she couldn't get comfortable, and her constant complaints very quickly began to irritate Frank. They hadn't lasted much longer. They had packed up and driven home in silence. That was one incident never to be repeated or discussed, but they had enjoyed many a stroll along a riverbank, promenade or pier, particularly on holiday. Over the years, their travels had taken them to some beautiful destinations. Liz could still recall the bitterness of the tiny cups of coffee they had been served in Italy, how they had 'played dodgems' with the traffic in Malta and the earnest young man in Egypt explaining the mysteries of Luxor. She wondered what had happened to his dreams and ambitions now.

They didn't do sunbathing, preferring to see the sites and immerse themselves in the local culture, but it was always nice to do so with a touch of sun on your back.

Having walked for ten minutes or so, Liz needed to sit down. Outside the small tourist information booth, a seat had been fashioned out of an old piece of timber. To one side were piles of lobster pots waiting to go out to sea with the morning fishermen. She sat with a thud. She wasn't the lightest of women and combined with her arthritic hips, sitting was no longer something she could do elegantly.

What a day! Liz couldn't quite believe how things had panned out. When she got up this morning and buttered her toast, she could not have anticipated that the day would have taken such an unexpected twist.

She had settled down to her morning programmes and would have still been in her comfy chair in front of the gas fire had it not been for running out of milk. What on earth had given her the idea of going into the café instead of the corner shop?

These days she wasn't one for sudden flights of fancy. Liz still couldn't quite comprehend what had prompted her to be so bold.

Perhaps it was destiny? If she believed in such things.

She was so pleased she had. She smiled as she uttered the name, Tom Beresford – after all these years and yet, this could complicate things. Being closer to her daughter and grandchildren was one thing, but she hadn't factored in a former lover.

Tom had been her first true love. Every school girl's dream – tall, dark and handsome. At 17, he was the tallest boy in the school. His dark hair styled in the latest fashion and the first flourish of a moustache caressed his top lip. She was smitten. She would see him at school in the morning assembly. The older boys would stand around the packed hall whilst the younger pupils filled up the rows of grey, plastic chairs. Each morning she would catch her breath as she cast around the uniformed bodies until she spotted him. Then just as quickly, she would turn away, scared he would notice her.

The first time they had talked had been at the youth club. Liz had gone along with her best friend, Audrey. They had been playing badminton when they were suddenly aware of being watched. Two boys had decided to venture into the sports hall, away from the juke box and wanted to know if they could join in. At first, the girls were too busy giggling to answer. If they let the boys play, would they drive them off the court and make fun of them, or was this an excuse to talk to them? They finally decided they would let them join in. Of course, it had just been a ruse, and ten minutes later, they were all drinking lemonade and giggling even more.

Liz didn't mind. Suddenly she was staring into the face of the boy that made her heart do cartwheels. They had talked all night until it had been time to go home and then every night after that. For 18 months, they had been inseparable until the day she boarded that bus to London.

It hadn't been easy to leave him, but she had managed to convince him that it was for the best. She had insisted that she would board the bus a single woman, and Tom was free to go and pursue his dream of joining the Navy and date someone else. That was the last she had seen of him, until today. Of course, Tom had always been on her mind, sheltering below everyday thoughts, but Liz had learnt to put his name out of her head and to get on with her life. Eventually, she had dedicated herself to Frank and Sarah and to making the best of what she had.

Was it Tom then that had enticed her into the café this morning, or was it just a massive coincidence that two people could both desire a drink and a slice of cake in the same place, at the same time, 50 years after they last saw each other?

The two hours they had spent together had passed in an instant. Liz couldn't remember the last time the minutes had gone so quickly. At home, time moved lethargically. Each passing minute seemed like an effort for the clock. She watched it endlessly and would swear it sometimes stopped, just to annoy her.

Her favourite television show lasted an hour, and that was the only time in the day when she wasn't conscious of each passing second and each twitch of the clock's hands. Whilst she was engrossed playing along with the contestants on the quiz show, she forgot the four walls of her living room. For a few precious moments, she was someone else. The clever one stood at the front of the class, answering the questions and building up her bank of gold stars.

The rest of the day was a different matter. Every 24 hours was a marathon. A battle of wits. What could she do to eat up the time? She read and cleaned, watched television and slept. Sleeping was one of the best ways she knew to fill a few hours. There was nothing she liked more than opening her eyes, sneaking a peek at her bedside alarm clock and seeing that a good couple of hours had disappeared.

It hadn't always been like this, but her world had altered beyond all recognition since Frank had died. Time had expanded. Suddenly she was aware of filling the gaps between getting up and going to bed, something she had never considered when Frank was in her life. Frank had been in control. She never felt dominated or bullied, but he had quietly asserted his authority over their life. He was not one for sitting down and relaxing. He always wanted to be doing. He rarely took it easy, whether working, making or mending something, going out for a drink or plotting their next adventure. He grabbed life by the shoulders and shook it into surrender. And then it all stopped. On that fateful day, that Monday morning when she had kissed his cheek and waved him off in the taxi to take him the short distance into town. He never came back. The policeman later told her that he died instantly and that he would not have suffered. She so wanted to believe that. The taxi had been hit head-on. It was all over in minutes, yet it opened a new, slower, more painful chapter of her life for Liz.

There were highlights, of course, such as when her daughter and grandkids came to visit. She loved to hear their voices and feel their youthful exuberance cascade through her home. When they dashed through the door, she was swept along in a wave of excitement. The void filled with laughter, and the clock blended into the background.

Spending time with them was pure joy. She thrived on their endless questions and thirst for answers. The girls had always loved to bake with her, and even now they were in their teens, it was still one of their favourite things to do when visiting Granny. When they baked together, she felt alive. Weighing out flour and mixing cake batter is so much fun when you are young that Liz didn't concern herself with the clouds of white dust engulfing her work surfaces or floor. What mattered at the moment was sharing her passion and seeing the children's delight when they opened the oven door to their golden confections.

Moving closer to her daughter had turned out to be a good thing, but it had been an enormous decision to leave the family home and all that was comforting and familiar. Liz had been alive to adventure in her youth, and she had gone places and done things that surprised her even now. Although she was an introvert at heart, she also had a determined, and some would say stubborn, side that refused to give up when she had set her mind to something. So she had gone to Germany alone as a young woman, taught in a foreign country, fallen in love with a local and enjoyed the most wonderful times.

Thirty plus years of marriage had done its best to change her. For the most part, she had succumbed to playing second fiddle to Frank. In the early days, she was attracted to his decisiveness. It was nice to be with someone who knew exactly what they wanted, but over time, she regretted not being able to have her say. It was mainly Frank who decided where they were going, what they were having for tea and when and where they would do the shopping. She dutifully tagged along. Carrying bags, making sure she had anticipated his every need, sunglasses, fold-up raincoat check. She didn't mind. They were generally happy and rubbed along alright. There wasn't much passion in the marriage, but they were content and didn't lack much.

Of course, there were days when she did feel taken for granted, and any time Frank suggested she couldn't do something – like drive the car – she was more determined than ever to prove him wrong. She had first tried in her early twenties, but it had ended in tears. It wasn't until Frank fell ill and needed someone to help him get to his hospital appointments that she had signed up for lessons and proved to herself and the rest of the street that she could indeed drive the car. Sadly even having passed her test, Frank still wasn't at ease with her in the driving seat. Whether it was nerves or chauvinistic pride, he couldn't help picking fault to the point where Liz flatly refused to drive him anywhere. So there they were with a brand new car on the drive and them taking a taxi to every hospital appointment.

Liz would take the car when she needed to get some shopping. She took advantage of the 24-hour supermarket opening hours to get there bright and early before the roads filled up with other drivers going off to work.

It was a small triumph and those few minutes spent in the car alone were special. It was the one time that Liz felt like an individual rather than simply Frank's wife.

It was losing Frank that had made her think about the woman she used to be. She still had a life to lead, and it was up to her now to decide how she wanted to spend her time. It would have been the easiest thing in the world to have stayed in the family home, but now alone, her options were limitless. Now it was time to decide how to spend her remaining years. The one thing she wanted more than anything was to be close to her daughter and to find her son. And so she had moved to Hainsborough.

*

After several minutes on the hard wooden seat, Liz felt the need to stand up. Easier said than done. The bit of exercise was already taking its toll on Liz's knees and hips. She winced as she stood up and slowly unfurled her body. She reached the corner shop and went in. It was stocked more for tourists than locals. As well as a fridge containing milk, water, juice and cans of pop were an endless assortment of items that would form the basis of a picnic or lunch on the beach. Shelves groaned with buckets and spades, inflatable animals and other such paraphernalia that families bought for days by the sea with the youngsters.

Liz bought the milk and turned to make the slow, now painful walk home. Twenty minutes later, she reached her front door, and boy was she ready for a cup of tea and maybe some biscuits.

Chapter Five

"Would you like some toast, Brenda love?" Asked Tom. "Yes, please, that would be lovely."

Tom smiled. Today had started well, and he felt optimistic for the day ahead. Brenda was up and dressed, and for now, at least, she seemed to recognise Tom and not be afraid of some stranger in her kitchen.

Outside, the sun was shining, and it looked like a good day for getting into the garden. They had both worked hard over the years to get the place looking just how they wanted it. Brenda loved flowers, and the borders around the ample lawn positively groaned with shrubs and plants, which ensured a colourful display all year long.

On good days even now, Brenda would wander into the garden, sometimes stopping to deadhead a rose or pull up an itinerant weed. Other days she would sit on the bench and stare into the distance.

It had been hard work. When the young couple first moved in, the garden was a mix of builder's rubble and clay. As a teenager, Brian had been pressed into service, helping to shift tons of earth and barrow in tons more top soil. Together they had laid a series of concrete paths and sectioned the garden into areas for growing vegetables, a rose garden, two lawns and the requisite deep borders.

Along the way, Tom had also accumulated a large

greenhouse, shed and workshop that the family had enjoyed at various stages of their childhood. His daughter Julie had commandeered the shed as a school for her and the other youngsters in the street. She had played for hours in there as the self-proclaimed teacher imposing her will over the others.

Later, Brian spent time in the workshop with his dad learning how to make and mend the full range of household appliances before hitting driving age when cars and motorbikes demanded his attention.

Tom loved it. There was nothing that gave him more pleasure than spending time with his son, covered in muck and grease, imparting his knowledge and seeing his boy develop from a boy to a man. And now he had the grandkids—a chance to do it all over again.

"I thought I might get Daniel to help me cut the lawn," said Tom as he joined Brenda at the table where she had set out their breakfast.

"I thought you could keep an eye on Archie. He's no bother. He'll probably have his head stuck in a book."

Brenda was no longer listening, transfixed with buttering her toast.

Moments later, there was a brief knock on the door followed by excited voices and the sound of the boys running through the front door.

"Boys!" Shrieked Cheryl, "Settle down."

Their mum appeared in the living room doorway, laden down with coats and bags. Her fully made-up face couldn't hide the tired look in her eyes. She dropped the bags on the nearest sofa and let herself drop down next to them.

"Grandad", Daniel rushed at Tom, giving him a big hug before doing the same to Brenda. At the sound of the door opening, she was back in the room, her face beaming. She loved the boys, and a visit from them always seemed to do the trick.

"Hello boys", she said. "Have you had your breakfast? What about a nice bit of toast and jam?" Not waiting for the answer, Brenda was up and making her way to the kitchen. Food was always the way Brenda showed affection. She loved to cook and bake and always ensured the house was full of treats for the children and visitors.

Brian used to love the smell of his mother's baking when he arrived home from school. The air filled with delicious aromas of baked fruit, cinnamon and almonds. The pantry would be stacked with tins containing cake, lemon curd tarts, currant slices and the family favourite, Bakewell Tart.

One of life's disappointments to Brian was that his wife Cheryl didn't have his mum's prowess in the kitchen. He ought not to complain as she had many other talents, but still, he couldn't help thinking how nice it would be to come home after a hard day at work to a freshly baked pie.

"Sorry about that," said Cheryl. "I'm afraid the boys are rather excited. We said we would take them away for a few days at half term if they behave themselves."

"Just give me a minute to check how your mum is doing with that toast. We don't want the alarm going off if she leaves it in too long. Just be a sec."

Tom rescued the toast just in time and popped it on a plate for Brenda, who was absent-mindedly looking out of the window. She seemed miles away. Tom wondered what it must be like for his beautiful, intelligent wife to be reduced to this. His heart ached when he saw how easily distracted she could be, no longer able to concentrate on this simplest of tasks like making toast. He comforted himself with the thought that she was not aware of her plight and was instead lost in a new world.

"Hello Brian, Cheryl love, are you stopping for a cup of tea?" Brenda put the pile of buttered toast in the middle of the table. "We won't, thanks, Brenda," said Cheryl. "We need to be going, and we don't want to be late for our appointment in town."

"Oh, we've got time for a quick cuppa, and I rather fancy a piece of that toast", contradicted Brian.

"Well, there's plenty to go round and tea in the pot."

Cheryl bit her lip. She was sick of being ignored, but this was neither the time nor place to say anything, so she just smiled instead and noted the incident in her increasingly bulging mental file marked Brian.

Ten minutes or so later, Brian stood up from the

table and acknowledged that now it was time that he and his wife headed into town.

"We shouldn't be too long. A couple of hours max."

"It doesn't matter, son. The boys are fine here, and we'll all be fine."

As soon as the front door closed, Archie went straight to one of the bags dumped on the sofa. He pulled out his Walkman and earphones, plugged himself in and made himself comfortable. That would be him for the next half an hour at least.

Brenda and Tom smiled and exchanged knowing glances.

"Did dad say what they were going to town for?" Asked Daniel half-heartedly as he settled himself on his granddad's lap.

"No. He just asked if we were OK to mind you two for a couple of hours. I can't imagine it's anything fascinating, and they are probably looking at carpets or new kitchens. Now then, Daniel lad, will you give your old granddad a hand to cut the lawn?

Daniel nodded. He was a boy of a few words, and as he was a few years off becoming a teenager, Tom could only imagine that it would get worse, not better, for the foreseeable future.

"Come on then." The two disappeared off to the shed, leaving Brenda with the breakfast things.

That is how it had always been. She cooked and cleaned and did the washing up, and when Tom was home from sea, he mended things. How

Brenda coped with running the household when he wasn't there never seemed to occur to Tom. Brenda was far more capable than he ever gave her credit for. She never said anything. It wasn't worth it. She was happy to have him home, and it was more important to create a comfortable family atmosphere than cause any upset.

"Grandma, can you help me with my school project?" Archie, bored with listening to music, was now standing in the kitchen with a large blue box he had fetched from the bedroom.

"Of course, darling? What is it?"

"It's a family tree. We have to talk to people like grannies and granddads and find out about their mummies and daddies. Then we have to draw it all on a big tree. We can include photographs and pictures to show what it was like to live in the olden days. You have lots of photographs, don't you?"

"Well, we have some. Not everyone had a camera when I was little, but I do have the odd photo of your great grandparents."

"Will you show me?" "Let's sit at the table.

The blue box used to house a canteen of cutlery. Brenda thought it might even have been a wedding present. Inside, a mass of black and white photographs mixed in with wallets containing colour prints and albums featuring treasured family holidays.

All the grandchildren, just like Brian and Julie before them, had always enjoyed rummaging through the snaps. Although Archie himself had seen the pictures before, he didn't seem to remember them. The school project looked to be focusing his attention this time as he randomly picked up images from the sea in front of him.

"Who is this lady? She looks very cross?" Asked Archie.

"That was my mum, Joyce Rose. She isn't cross in the picture. Everyone in those days looked serious when they were having their photo taken."

"Was she nice?"

"She could be. We had to be very well behaved, and we couldn't run around and shout, but we generally had a nice childhood. "I'll write her name here on the piece of paper, above your name," Archie added a thick blue crayon line linking her to her mother.

"Now, she married Malcolm, your great granddad. He was a printer. You would have liked him. He was funny, and he always had butterscotch in his pocket."

The piece of paper was filling up nicely when granddad and Daniel came back into the room. Daniel looked at the tree and the photos that were placed next to the names.

"Why are there no photos of my dad as a baby?" Daniel enquired casually but somewhat astutely as it turned out.

Tom noticed Brenda wince. It was one of those innocuous-sounding questions, but it cut her to the quick. Tom stepped in.

"Well, we've probably told you before, but your dad and auntie Julie were adopted. Your dad was five when he came to us, and there weren't any photos of him before then. This picture here next to his name is the first one that we took. He was a happy young man." Tom explained.

"Well, he would be happy coming to live with you."

"Oh, that's a nice thing to say. Thank you, Daniel.

"So, does dad know who his real mum and dad are?" Continued Daniel.

"I don't think so. You'd have to ask your dad. Growing up, he always said that we were his mum and dad, which was all that mattered. I don't know that he has ever tried to find out anything more."

"Must be odd, not knowing where you came from or anything about your parents. They could be anybody, Einstein or a mass murderer."

"Well, Einstein couldn't be his father, but I know what you mean. Thankfully your dad doesn't seem to remember much about his life before he came to us, and it doesn't seem to have been a big issue for him. He's had plenty of love, and that's all that matters. Now, what about some tea and cake?"

Brenda didn't seem aware of the pain now, but it had been the source of much sorrow for the newlyweds that they couldn't produce a baby of their own. Each, in turn, had blamed themselves and whilst the marriage had been strong enough to withstand the disappointment, adoption had been a welcome yet heart wrenching decision.

Tom was sure that he was the reason they couldn't conceive. He had felt emasculated not to produce a son and heir and had over compensated by spoiling the two new additions to the family at every opportunity.

They had ended up travelling halfway across the country to collect Brian. In those days, you couldn't adopt on your doorstep, and for some reason or other, they had eventually been offered a child from an orphanage in Chester. The adoption service had advised them not to expect a baby, as they were in heavy demand, so they had agreed to see the five-year-old boy.

Brenda had been glad that he was the first child that they had met. She hated the thought of trying to decide between one child and the next. In that situation, it became more like a beauty contest, and she couldn't stand the thought of making such a life-changing decision on something so shallow.

Brian was a lovely boy. Dark hair and deep brown eyes, a small birthmark on his right cheek. They used to call it his strawberry when he was little, but it wasn't that well defined. She had been taken by how similar his colouring was to Tom's, something she saw as a massive bonus as growing up, Brian never looked out of place, and the topic of his adoption had come up surprisingly infrequently.

He was quiet when he first came to them and gave no hint of having memories of life in the orphanage, and they just hoped he wasn't repressing anything too awful to contemplate. Very quickly, he settled in and by the time he started big school, he was a confident and lovable young man.

They had waited until Brian was about Daniel's age before they broached the matter with him. He was 12 when his best friend Josh learned that his dad was not the man currently in a relationship with his mum. Josh was reeling from the news and had taken to sleeping over at their house, finding comfort in what he thought was a 'normal' family. It was then that Brian had started to ask questions, and of course, they couldn't lie. "Poor Josh, fancy finding out that the guy you have known all your life isn't your father after all. I'd better just check; you are my father, aren't you?" Brian had asked Tom, almost in jest.

It was the most challenging conversation of their life. They had looked at each other, and that moment's hesitation had been enough to send Brian into a tailspin.

"No, you have got to be joking. Why wouldn't you tell me before?" Brian was crying uncontrollably, and his shoulders were heaving with each sob.

"We have been waiting for the right moment. We wanted you to be old enough to understand, and up to now, it has never felt appropriate."

"but now Josh's life has been ripped apart; you thought you would do the same to me? So who is my real dad then?"

"Honestly, son. We don't know. You were placed in an orphanage when you were just a baby. Your mum was young and felt that you would have a better life with a family that could give you more than she could as a single mother. We don't know much more than that.

"We adopted you when you were five years old and have loved you as our son from the day we set eyes on you. I know this is a terrible shock, but I hope, in time, you won't let this come between us."

The next few weeks had been tough. Brian had become withdrawn and avoided them at every opportunity. Tom and Brenda were wracked with guilt. Had they left it too late? Should they have told him when he was in primary school? Would he ever forgive them?

Gradually things settled down. Josh took comfort from the idea that his dad was a famous rock star who had left him because he was heading off on a world tour. Brian, on the other, had just accepted that Tom was one hell of a dad and that he didn't think anyone could come close.

Thankfully the topic didn't come up again, and life returned to as normal as it ever had been, apart from when Julie came along.

Brian was not impressed when they had first floated the idea of him having a little sister. He would have rather had a puppy.

Once he saw her, though, he had immediately assumed the mantel of protective big brother, although Julie herself hadn't been as easy to please.

Julie had been a handful. The teenage years, in particular, had been long and painful. Brenda had often remarked when they were tucked up in bed how much she loved her daughter but at the same time disliked her intensely.

"It's a phase." Tom would say. "She'll grow out of it. Deep down, she is a good girl, and she just sees how far she can push things."

She had continued to push the boundaries. She refused to do her A levels, deciding to leave school at 16 and take a job in the local sewing factory. She had endless partners over the years and finally, at 30, got pregnant, allegedly by choice, insisting that she was keeping the baby and wanted nothing more to do with the child's father.

Tom and Brenda had been to hell and back with her. However, she had proved herself to be an attentive mother, and she had done an excellent job at making a loving home in which to raise her son, Zane. The baby's name itself was another source of contention.

"What kind of name is that to give a baby?" Brenda had asked rhetorically. Julie would always have the last word.

"It's the name I've chosen for my baby." She had replied emphatically.

Five years on, Tom and Brenda loved the very bones of young Zane and could forgive their daughter for most things, having given them such a beautiful grandchild. Julie had progressed up the ranks at the factory and was now a manager. She earned a decent wage and no longer gave her parents much concern. Of course, they did worry – that's what they did best, but all in all, Julie didn't cause too much anxiety.

Chapter Six

Brian and Cheryl didn't speak on the drive from Tom's house to their appointment in town. Brian gripped the steering wheel tightly, his steely gaze fixed on the road ahead and his mouth set in a thin colourless line.

Cheryl, who always sat bolt upright in any seat, was staring at her fingers. She picked idly at the bright red nail varnish that was starting to peel away at the cuticles. The sooner this is over, the better, she thought.

Brian manoeuvred into a parking space at the back of the tall, grey building, and the pair got out. A receptionist greeted them as they entered the building.

"Mr and Mrs Beresford," Brian said, addressing the young woman.

She looked down at the list in front of her and then said, "Ah yes, you have an appointment with Ms Lane. Please take the lift to the third floor, and she will meet you up there."

Brian put a hand in the small of his wife's back and gently ushered her towards the lift. Cheryl visibly twitched but said nothing.

Ms Lane was waiting to meet them as the lift doors opened. She was dressed professionally in a charcoal tailored suit, a white blouse, sky-high heels, and a beaming smile.

"Hello, Mr and Mrs Beresford, pleased to meet

you, please come this way."

She led them into a brightly lit office. Brian wasn't sure quite what he was expecting, but somehow the room seemed more cheerful than he might have imagined. Tall vases of expensive-looking flowers adorned various surfaces, and the bland artwork on the walls reminded him of the type of paintings you see in hotel rooms.

Ms Lane invited them to sit on a large sofa, and she took a seat opposite them. A jug of water and three glasses, and an ominous box of tissues sat on the low coffee table between them.

"Hello, my name is Claire. Are you happy if I call you Brian and Cheryl?"

Brian and Cheryl nodded.

"Before we get started, I'll just outline a little bit about how the sessions will run and what you can expect. Can I just ask, has either of you had any counselling before?"

For the first time in a couple of hours, Cheryl spoke.

"I have. I had some bereavement counselling after my sister died. We are talking 15 years ago, though."

"But you found it helpful?" Claire enquired calmly. "Yes. Very."

"So I take it this is your first time, Brian? How are you feeling?" Claire's gaze turned to Brian, and he felt flush.

"Well, a bit nervous, I suppose. I am not sure what to expect, and I am not the world's best about talking about my feelings, but I am here to give it a go." He shifted uneasily in his seat.

For the next few minutes, Claire explained the theory of Cognitive Behavioural Therapy and how she ran her sessions. She wasn't there to come up with solutions, and they would only get out as much as they put in. Brian was already on the verge of zoning out from the clichés, but the more Claire talked, the less he would have to, so he was smiling and nodding as she spoke, willing her to continue. All too soon, though, the questions started in earnest.

"So, what has brought you here today?"

The question hung in the air for a while like a spray from an aerosol. Directionless. Then suddenly, it landed on Cheryl, and she was off.

"Brian has been having an affair. He says it is over and that he is sorry and wants me to forgive him, but if we are going to make a go of things, we need to reconnect, which means opening up about what is going on with each of us. It was my idea to come to counselling, and I hope it helps; otherwise, we might have to go our separate ways, and I don't want that for the children."

Brian flushed deeper. Was it normal to feel embarrassed, he wondered, and why was he? It was true Claire was rather attractive. Would she think less of him now she knew he was the unfaithful kind? Again, most people who passed through this office and sat on these seats must be guilty of similar wrongdoings.

"Can you tell me a little more, Cheryl? When did you find out about the affair, and how has it affected you? Claire was pushing at an open door. Cheryl was desperate to talk.

"I've known for about a month. There were the classic tell-tale signs, the working late, unexpected trips away on business. We hadn't been intimate for a long time, and one night I had had enough of feeling invisible, so I asked him outright if there was someone else. At least he had the courtesy of telling me the truth.

"I was hurt and shocked. Even though I was brave enough to ask the question, I hadn't prepared myself for the answer. Brian is a great dad, and I can't bear the thought of us splitting up and putting the boys through all that pain."

"Thank you, Cheryl. I realise this is painful for you, but the more you and Brian open up, the better the sessions will be. So, Brian, can you tell me what led you to have an affair?"

Brian shuffled. Where to start?

"As Cheryl said, we haven't been intimate for a while, and I suppose I was flattered when someone else paid me attention. At first; it was just about sex, and then I started to have feelings for the other person. I love Cheryl, but I sometimes find our relationship a bit claustrophobic, and I just enjoyed feeling a bit freer."

Brian was careful not to mention Cath's name, as he didn't want to cause Cheryl any more hurt if that was possible.

Claire was silent. The pregnant pause stretched out like a tight washing line between them. It was like a childish game, who could keep quiet the longest.

Brian cracked. "I never intended to hurt anyone", another cliché he thought, but it was true.

Cheryl's was staring at her fingers.

"I was caught up in the moment. I never stopped to think about what would happen if anyone found out. It was like I was in a parallel universe. When I wasn't with Cheryl, I didn't give my home life a second thought. I don't mean that negatively. I was just in the moment oblivious to normal life.'

Brian thought how lame this all sounded now he was saying it out loud. When he was with Cath, he was in the moment and didn't give home life a second thought.

They had enjoyed each other's company. They talked nonstop, laughed, had meals out and drinks in places he wouldn't ordinarily go to, and it had all been pleasurable. The sex had been good too, and whilst it was a definite bonus, it was the whole package that made it so compelling. Perhaps it was because Cath came without baggage. When he was with her, Brian was just Brian; he wasn't a husband or father. They didn't have to talk about school or football practice. They had grown-up fun. Being at Cath's house was a more relaxing experience generally than being at home. Cath didn't nag him to take his shoes off the sofa or put a coaster under his cup.

Cheryl found Brian's candour hard to stomach. Whilst finding out your husband was having sex with someone else was terrible enough, knowing they were enjoying good times whilst she was at home with the kids made it ten times worse. Having intimate conversations, laughing and joking seemed somehow more personal than just exchanging bodily fluids. Given that she wasn't keeping him satisfied in bed, she could come to terms with someone else fulfilling that need, but the thought that Cath – she hated her already – was the better company was harder to bear.

Before today she had not been as aware of Brian's depth of feeling for this other woman. She was pleased they had agreed to do the counselling as with this revelation, there was no way they would make it on their own. She wasn't sure how she would get through this particular chapter, but she had to. She was determined to keep their marriage on track and not just for the boys. She loved Brian and didn't want to lose him. It wouldn't be easy to forgive him, and she didn't know how long it would take before things got back to normal, but the fact that they were both here today at least gave her reassurance that they were both willing to try.

Then it was over. The session had hardly got going, but that was it—time to pack all the rawness and upset away for another week. Brian and Cheryl shook Claire's hand and left the office.

"That was pretty intense. How about we grab a coffee and have a chat about how we are going to handle things when we get home?" suggested Brian.

"Good idea," said Cheryl.

Brian was amazed that she had agreed. Perhaps the session had been worthwhile after all. He would take this as a positive first step. As they turned the corner outside, they spotted a Costa and decided that would do nicely.

Cheryl found a couple of seats towards the back of the café whilst Brian queued. Moments later, they savoured their flat whites and shared a lemon muffin that Brian had bought spontaneously. Cheryl didn't feel like eating, but she didn't want to appear churlish and start an argument, so she feigned interest in the bun.

"What did you think of the session? Was it anything like you had imagined?" Asked Cheryl between mouthfuls.

"It was more challenging in some respects. As I said in there, I want to be honest, but at the same time, I don't want to rub your nose in things and make the situation any worse. I know how much I have hurt you, and I don't want you to be hurt all over again every time we discuss details of what I have been up to. I know it sounded corny in there, but I was telling the truth when I said it was like I was operating in a parallel universe.

"The main thing that concerns me is that we can be civil to one another and put on a united front for the boys and mum and dad. The last thing any of them needs is to think something is wrong or to feel any tension between us. Don't you think?"

"I agree, of course, I do, but at the same time, it is hard to pretend everything is OK. The boys are not daft, and they can sense when things aren't right, but as far as they are concerned, it's just a silly argument and nothing to worry about. All we can do is try and keep coming back to see Claire.

"I noticed, by the way..."

"What?"

"The way you looked at her," and there it was. Just as Brian thought they were going to end on a positive note. This was a test he was sure of it. He could take the bait and go off into one of his rages, or he could simply smile and change the subject. He chose the latter course of action but filed it away for later.

Ten minutes later, they were heading back to pick up the boys.

Chapter Seven

Liz wasn't one for joining clubs or taking up hobbies that would involve her sitting in a classroom with a load of strangers. Odd then that she had agreed to accompany her neighbour to the community hall where the local college offered a painting workshop. Generally, Liz hated people telling her what to do, even if she was there to learn.

Going to school had been a challenge for her. She wasn't particularly academic, but neither was she musical or sporty. She was just average - at everything. Of all the subjects, it was geography that stirred her imagination. She felt that learning about other countries might be helpful to her, and she longed to travel. Growing up in a small town only made her more determined to spread her wings at the first opportunity. She rather liked the idea of being an air hostess or a journalist.

Something that would involve her moving from country to country. She was as surprised as her parents when she finally settled on nursing as a career. If she was honest with herself even now, she wasn't sure whether it was just the chance to go to London that had sealed the deal on her chosen career. Had she not been pregnant at the time, she imagined she would have made much more of her months in the capital. She would have loved to have gone to more shows and spent more time enjoying the sights. As it was, she had her nose stuck in a textbook most nights, and with no money to spare, she hardly saw outside of her digs.

Since losing her husband, Liz knew it was important that she made an effort to make some new friends. That is why she had agreed to go along to the painting class as a ploy to get to know her neighbour, Katie, a little better, and as someone relatively new to the delights of painting, she did think she might learn a thing or two.

Katie was a similar age to Liz, and she, too, was widowed. Having had five years more than Liz to get used to the idea of being on her own again, Katie was the queen of new experiences. From the day she was bereaved, she had embraced her life with renewed vigour. She was open to trying every experience that she could find. Her husband's untimely death reminded her how precious life is, and Katie was determined not to waste another minute of it. Her zest for life was just what Liz needed. She was like a breath of fresh air blowing away the cobwebs and the remnants of her life with Frank and ushering in a new era of possibilities. If it hadn't been for meeting Katie, Liz thought she would be spending her days languishing at home, with the highlight of the day being her favourite programme on television.

As it turned out, they had laughed at the workshop and learned a few things. Katie was a real giggler, and they had been like two naughty school girls sitting at the back of the class. She was delighted with what she had picked up, and the session had inspired her to do more. She might even invest in some brushes and paints and have a go at home. There was certainly no shortage of lovely views not far from her home. She could quite easily walk out to the cliff tops and paint.

The workshop had also been a good way for Liz to meet more of her neighbours. They were a friendly bunch. Perhaps now she was single, she might make an effort to be more sociable. One couple had already invited her round for a coffee or glass of wine, and she must follow it up rather than leaving it as just some pleasantry that people uttered out of politeness.

After the workshop, Katie had dragged Liz into a nearby pub and had presented her with a cocktail, complete with Maraschino cherry and kitsch paper umbrella. Despite protesting at the idea of drinking at such an hour, Liz had enjoyed the Cosmopolitan and was secretly delighted to be adding yet another first to her list. If she stuck with Katie, who knew what she would do next?

It was after the second cocktail that Liz found herself telling Katie all about Tom. Katie was beside herself with excitement. She was only too keen to search out male company, and the thought that Liz had found her second Mr Right and had a chance to rekindle her childhood romance was the stuff of dreams. Katie implored Liz to keep her informed at every step in her burgeoning relationship. She wanted a blow by blow account of her subsequent encounter with Tom.

Liz was also excited at the prospect of meeting up with Tom again. She had been pleasantly surprised how well their first encounter had gone, to say it was such a bolt out of the blue for both of them. At 18, she had left him in difficult circumstances; she had hurt him and was sorry. His first reaction to seeing her after nearly half a century could have been very different. Time must have helped to heal any wound. She was glad. She was amazed he even recognised her. She had filled out since he had last seen her. Her hair nor her figure had any resemblance to that of the young, slender woman he had waved off.

They had been good friends, soul mates, but that was when they were teenagers. Could she hope that they could rediscover the affection they felt for each other all those years ago? She wondered if she should even be thinking this way, given Frank was barely cold in the ground. She was only after a friend though, she wasn't thinking she would become the second Mrs Beresford - presuming Tom had had just the one wife.

Fancy, she thought, him in the Navy. She imagined how dashing he would have looked in his uniform. He had gone to sea soon after she had left. She hoped he had found comfort in his chosen career, and yes, she couldn't help wondering if he had found comfort in the arms of anyone else. She hadn't. Not for a long time after she had left. She was so traumatized at having got pregnant after just one night with Tom that she couldn't face the prospect of anyone else touching her. She had focused on her career and put the thought of men out of her mind until the day she met Frank. She was grown up then, and their relationship was different from the first rush of love she had felt as a teenager.

Tom and Liz had agreed that they would see each other again on Wednesday. Whilst Liz loved the idea of them being keen to rekindle their friendship. However, she found the idea of meeting up with Tom slightly disconcerting. He was married, after all.

Whilst she understood that Tom's wife had dementia, Liz still felt uncomfortable doing things behind her back. There was also the matter of her own family and what she would say and when to tell her daughter that she was seeing another man.

Chapter Eight

Liz had hardly slept on Tuesday night as the anticipation built for her meeting with Tom. She wasn't sure what was keeping her awake most, the excitement of seeing him again or the prospect of what she had to tell him.

She was up and dressed by 7 am. She couldn't decide what to wear. She wanted to make an effort, but then she didn't want to look out of place in the cafe. Last week, she wore slacks and a blouse which ordinarily she wouldn't wear outside the house. This time she settled on a lovely brown skirt, crisp white blouse and light cardigan. She put on some make-up and a pair of neat earrings and paid extra attention to her hair. She still had a thick mop, and although it was now predominantly grey, she took pride in having it cut and styled at regular intervals. Her blue eyes were bright, and her glasses stylish.

'I'll do', she thought. Never one for overconfidence.

Eventually, it was time to leave. Liz was the first to arrive at the cafe. She ordered a cup of tea and her favourite slice of Bakewell Tart and sat at the table in the corner. She wondered whether Tom always sat in the same seat. Her stomach was churning. She felt as nervous as that fateful day when she left Tom standing at the bus station waving her goodbye.

Tom arrived at 12.30 pm. He smiled when he saw Liz, got himself a drink and joined her at the table.

"I'm pleased you are here," he said, looking relieved.

"Why wouldn't I be?"

"Oh, I don't know. I have been thinking of all sorts since last week. Perhaps you had seen enough or wish you had never laid eyes on me again. Anyway, I am glad you are here. Have you been up to much since I last saw you?"

"I did go to a painting lass at the community centre, which was fun, and I met a few of the neighbours, but that's been about it. I am not very adventurous. To be honest, I wouldn't usually even go in a cafe on my own; that is why last week was such a shock."

Tom was hanging on her every word. He was mesmerised, transported back in time. He felt like a teenager.

"Painting? Is that your hobby then?"

"No, well, that was the point. I haven't done any painting before, and I've never been a big one for hobbies. I used to knit when Sarah was little, but nowadays, the kids don't appreciate homemade clothes. I just thought it might be a way to meet some people."

"Good idea. I'm not the only one from school that has ended up here. Do you remember Bob Wright, a skinny, ginger-haired kid in our year? He used to get into loads of fights. Well, he's in Hainsborough with his wife, and I'll tell you who else you might

63

remember Sarah Montague; you were quite good friends with her, weren't you?"

"Good grief. Talk about a small world. How did you find them?"

"Again, just chance. I met Bob with his missus in Tesco of all places, and I think Sarah I saw in the library. She's looking well. She moved with her husband when they retired. They have one of the nice flats on North Bay. Pricey they are, so they must be worth a bob or two. We'll have to see if we can track them down. It would be fun to meet up and go over the good old days."

"Is that how you think of them, the good old days? I didn't think you were that keen on school?"

"Well, they were a damn sight easier than working for a living. I'd give anything to be as carefree now as I was then."

As he was speaking, Tom was thinking about the stress he felt looking after Brenda. He had not known anything as challenging as the last few months.

"So, what stops you from feeling carefree now? Retirement is supposed to be all about 'me time', isn't it? You've raised your family and paid off the mortgage, so you are free to enjoy yourself." Liz made it all sound so simple.

"Well, the first few years after I retired from the Navy, the wife and I enjoyed some good times, but then she got sick, and that took the shine off things. These days I get lonely, and of course, you never stop worrying about the kids, however old they are. I am worried about my son, Brian. I am not sure what is going on, but things aren't going that well at home. I'm worried he's having some marital issues. His wife, Cheryl, is a bit of a funny one. I find her quite uptight."

"I know what you mean about never stopping worrying. Tell me a bit more about Brian."

"He's adopted. That's been the hardest thing I have had to come to terms with all my life."

Liz flushed. She was taken aback by Tom's revelation, but she also felt privileged that he felt comfortable enough to open up to her.

"I couldn't quite come to terms with the fact that we couldn't have children of our own. It was a massive disappointment. You kind of take it for granted as newlyweds that you'll have a family. We didn't bother going for tests as we didn't want the responsible one to feel guilty, so I suppose we both carried the guilt. I have spent my whole married life feeling like I let Brenda down by not being able to give her a child."

"So, eventually, we decided to adopt. We ended up going to Chester, of all places, to an orphanage to see Brian. He was five years old. Gorgeous young lad. Dark hair and eyes and long eyelashes. Love at first sight, I suppose you would say. We brought him home, and that was that. I loved him like my own from day one.

"He was no trouble growing up, and he has turned into a wonderful young man. Well, I say young; he's 36 now. He is married, as I said, and he has two boys of his own, Daniel and Archie. Both of them are the spitting image of Brian as a young lad. They live close enough that we get to see plenty of the grandkids."

"Look at me monopolising the conversation. I have hardly let you get a word in edgewise."

"Not at all," reassured Liz "it's lovely to hear your story. We have an awful lot to catch up on. It's hard to know where to start. It sounds like Brian dropped on being adopted by you and Brenda. I just hope Christopher was as lucky."

And just like that, the words had left Liz's mouth. After half a century of never uttering his name out loud, she had let slip the one name that meant things would never be the same again.

Inevitably, Tom asked the following question without missing a beat.

"Who is Christopher?"

"Oh, Tom, I shouldn't have said that. This is going to come as an awful shock. Christopher is my, our son, and I am afraid I haven't been frank with you. When I left for London, I was pregnant, and mum and Dad were outraged and about to disown me. They shipped me off to my Auntie Doris."

Tom was ashen. He could not believe what he was hearing. It was like a searing arrow to his heart. The pain was so intense he wondered whether it was a heart attack. His head was spinning, and his hands felt clammy.

"I wanted to tell you, but my parents wouldn't

hear of it. They were scared stiff I would be the talk of the village and disgrace the family. They sent me to live with Auntie Doris until the baby was born. I was heartbroken. I loved you very much, and all I wanted was for us to have the baby and get married, but of course, I was too young, and it wasn't the done thing to be a single mum at just 17."

"What happened to the baby?"

"I had a boy, Christopher. I thought he was the most beautiful thing I had ever seen. I only got to hold him for a few moments before they took him away and put him for adoption. It was the worst day of my life, and I cried for weeks. I have never stopped thinking about him. I didn't have a choice, but I have never stopped feeling guilty for letting him go. I am so sorry, Tom, that you never knew."

As she reached for a tissue to mop her face, Liz noticed she wasn't the only one shedding tears.

"I can't believe it. I have a son. My flesh and blood. Oh, Liz."

"I am sorry, Tom. This must be a huge shock. I have been wondering whether I should tell you all week, but I didn't mean to blurt it out. I have kept it a secret for so long. I am relieved to tell you finally. I never told Frank, and my daughter doesn't know yet either."

"What do you mean yet? Are you planning to tell her?" Tom was unsure where things were going.

"After Frank died, I decided that now was the time I should try and find Christopher. I have thought of nothing else, and if there is any chance that I could find him and explain things to him, I want to do that. I know it won't be easy, but I can't go to my grave not having tried."

"How do you even start to find him?"

Tom was not at all convinced that this was the right thing to do.

"I think it depends whether he wants to meet his biological parents. I haven't made that many inquiries yet, but if the child wants to know, you can give the Adoption Service your contact details to pass on. What do you think, Tom, should we find our son?"

It was a few moments before Tom was able to reply. Having just heard the biggest bombshell of his life, he was also conscious that he had to be getting home. His time was nearly up, and Brian would be expecting him home, but how could he leave?

"Liz, I know this is the most inappropriate moment to walk away, but I do have to go. Not because of anything you have said, but Brian is waiting for me at home, and I need to get back. If I had a choice, I would stay and talk some more. I know it can't have been easy carrying around that secret for all these years, and I do thank you for letting me know. Can we see each other again next week and continue the conversation?"

Before she could say any more, Tom stood up to leave, and as he fastened his coat, he bent forward and planted a soft kiss on Liz's cheek. He smiled weakly, turned and left.

It was only then that Liz realised how full the cafe had become in the time they had been sitting by the window. They had each made one drink last nearly an hour, and they had been so engrossed in conversation they were oblivious to the other customers coming and going around them. The girl who had served them was clearing the tables, and when she caught Liz's eye, she commented: "Looks like you were having a fairly serious conversation, so I left you to it. Are you ready for another cuppa?"

"Yes, please, that would be lovely."

Liz was in turmoil. She felt if she stood up, her legs might buckle beneath her. Had she done the right thing telling Tom? Had the shock been too much for him? What would happen now? She needed to sit for a little longer and gather her thoughts before she could even think about walking home.

Chapter Nine

Tom's head was spinning. As he made his way home, he cursed himself for leaving Liz at such an essential point in their conversation. He didn't want to go, but if he didn't get back, Brian would start worrying, and he didn't like to take advantage of him; if he began to stretch the hour too much, Brian might decide to stop offering to do it, and it was too important to Tom to miss.

Oh my goodness, thought Tom. I have a son. All this time, there has been an unknown part of me out in the world. All those years of heartache thinking I could not father a child, and I already had one. He had so many questions. So many thoughts. He could do with sitting down and trying to make sense of it all. He mustn't let on at home, though. As far as Brian and Brenda were concerned, he had just popped out for a stroll; they didn't need to know about his rendezvous with Liz.

"Dad, at last, where have you been?" The questions were coming thick and fast as Brian greeted his father on the threshold. He looked worried.

"Why? What's going on?"

"It's mum; she's wandered off."

"What do you mean? I thought you were here to look after her; what do you mean, wandered off?" Tom had not meant for his question to be accusatory, but Brian was feeling guilty.

"I was in the kitchen with the radio on. I was preparing a salad for lunch. Mum was in the garden pottering around. I popped out to see if she wanted a drink, and she wasn't there. The back gate was open, and she had disappeared. I had a quick look up and down the street, but I couldn't see her. I don't know how long she has been gone. Where would she go? Do you think we should call the police?" Brian was panicking.

"I think it is a bit too soon for that. Your mum might come back at any moment. Why don't you ring Julie and check she hasn't gone to hers and I'll ring round a few of the neighbours. Then we'll go and have a look round."

Tom heard his son on the phone to his daughter. Julie would be at work, and he could only imagine the stress that receiving such a phone call would induce in her. Julie was calm and practical by nature, she would instinctively know what to do, but all the same, the call would be a bolt out of the blue.

Poor Brenda, he thought. What state of mind was she in today? She had been quite lucid at breakfast and had settled as usual into the morning routine. She had recognised Brian when he arrived, and all the signs were positive. Had she set he mind on going somewhere, or had she aimlessly wandered out of the garden? It was a long time since she had gone anywhere alone, and Tom wasn't sure she would know where she was. He started to feel nauseous. Brian came back into the living room.

"Julie is going to go home and check if mum has turned up, and then she will come over here.

She said it would be best if one of us stays here and the others go out to have a look round."

"That sounds like a plan. I'll make a few calls to see if anyone has seen your mum. She can't have gone far."

A few minutes later, Tom returned to the living room. Brian was standing by the bay window looking out onto the street, his face contorted with worry. He looked older than his 36 years. Tom noticed the patch of grey hair at Brian's temples and the crow's feet that had appeared near his eyes. His boy was looking tired. He turned to acknowledge Tom:

"Anything?" Tom shook his head.

"No, nobody seems to have seen your mum pass by, but then, if they are like us, they probably spend most of their time in the living room at the back, rather than not looking out onto the street. Don't worry, son, I am sure we'll find her before long. She hasn't got her bag, so she has no money. She won't get far. Hopefully, she will make her way back before long." Brain didn't look convinced.

It was now nearly an hour since he had noticed his mum was no longer in the garden. That seemed a long time. After what seemed like another hour but wasn't, Julie arrived. She came bounding into the room, a coiled spring of energy. She gave her dad and brother a big hug.

"Don't worry, guys, we'll find mum before long. Dad, why don't you stay here in case mum comes back and Brian and I will have a drive round. Brian, you go left and go as far as the beach, and I'll go right and make a loop round past the bus station."

Brian couldn't argue with her no-nonsense approach. Often this way of speaking would drive him mad. Who was she to decide how things should be? Julie had a habit of telling people to do something rather than asking them. Growing up, he had often resented her forthrightness. Her bossiness was in stark contrast to his more measured approach. Secretly he had often wished he could be more like her, more decisive and articulate, but outwardly he had called her a bossy cow and tried to belittle her self-belief. Today though, there was no need for argument.

She was thinking clearly, and it felt suitable for someone else to be in charge of the situation. Brian would do what Julie said. He set off towards the beach.

Suddenly, Tom was alone. Loneliness was something he felt more and more these days. There were days when he hardly spoke.

Brenda didn't have much to say, and if she had a bad day where she didn't recognise him, Tom had learnt that it was best to say as little as possible, so he didn't upset her. At first, he had tried to correct her when she thought he was the doctor or a nurse, but now he knew better. He desperately missed the real Brenda, the one who used to sit and hold his hand and chat for hours. The one who would go dancing with him and out playing bowls. The one who would laugh at his jokes and listen to his rants when he disagreed with something on the news or in the paper. He missed his gorgeous wife, who would sit for hours patiently playing with the children or helping them with their homework. She was still beautiful. Her deep brown eyes and her gentle smile could still melt his heart.

Dementia was cruel. It was taking his Brenda away from him, and he hated it. He was gradually coming to terms with how things might pan out, but he had never considered life without her. This was the first time Tom had been alone in the house in well over six months. The silence, the empty chairs, the untouched food, the scenario weighed down on his chest like a huge rock, sapping his breath. He couldn't bear the thought that this was how it could be. Just him alone in the house. He might have days where he resented doing every little thing for Brenda, but they were the exception. Most days, he coped. Most days, he accepted his lot and did what he could for her with good grace. Anything is better than this, he thought. Then for the first time since getting home from the cafe, he felt genuine anxiety. Where was Brenda? Was she safe? Would she be back soon? It was all too much to bear.

Soon Brian and Julie were back home. They had

both drawn a blank. Julie had had to make a detour to go and collect Zane from school. He was too young to grasp what was going wrong, but the adults' tension was palpable, and even a five-year-old could work out something was amiss. He gave his granddad a big kiss.

"Where's grandma?" He asked innocently.

"We're not sure, lad," said Tom "she has gone for a walk, but we are not sure when she is coming back. Why don't you come over here and sit by your granddad? Tell me all about what you did at school today."

"Dad, I think we need to phone the police now. It's been nearly four hours since mum left." Brian was right.

Brenda was everything to Brian. He could still remember the pain he felt finding out about his adoption. It seemed impossible to belong to someone else. He even looked like Tom, and the thought that anyone but Brenda could have given birth to him appeared alien. Over the years, he had toyed with trying to track down his birth parents as much as anything so he could get a better idea of his family history and medical records. He was sick of going to the doctors and being asked what diseases and ailments ran in the family. It was times like that when he had a sense of being an outsider, an unknown. It was a very odd feeling. For most of the time, he felt he belonged to a close-knit, loving family, and it was only on those awkward occasions when it brought it home to him that he was an impostor.

He had never followed through trying to find his biological roots. He was scared of upsetting Brenda. He had wanted for nothing, and it seemed so unfair to go looking for someone who either didn't want him or couldn't look after him. So he had filed away those thoughts. Now Brenda was missing. He would never forgive himself if anything happened to her. He was supposed to be looking after her, taking care of her. How could he have been so stupid to let her out of his sight? He could not imagine life without her. She was the glue that bound the family together. Sure he loved his dad, but there was something special about his relationship with his mum. She understood him. She didn't try and make him into something he wasn't. She had supported him through tough times at school and gloried his successes at university. She was the reason he pushed himself and the one he wanted to please. She was his rock and his confidante.

Dementia had robbed him of some aspects of his mum. She didn't always know him these days, which was hard to bear, but she recognised the grandkids, which was a big relief. As long as Daniel and Archie could have a relationship with their grandma, he was happy. He still told her everything. It didn't matter whether she understood or not. When they were alone, Brian would sit by her side, hold her hand and tell her his troubles. It felt good to share, even if she could no longer soothe his brow or dispense words of comfort. He knew she was listening. He had told her all about the affair and the problems he was having at home. If she had been able to respond, she would have been hugely disappointed with him. She would have condemned his philandering and rebuked his loose morals, but she would also have listened patiently whilst he spilt his heart. She would ultimately have forgiven his misdemeanours, and she would do everything possible to help him see a way through his predicament. She was better than any counselling session.

Tom picked up the telephone and dialled 999. Was it an emergency, he wondered? He didn't want some wet behind the ears young police officer telling him off for wasting police time. It had been four hours, though, and that was an awfully long time for Brenda to be out in the streets alone. Within half an hour, a police officer arrived at the house.

Tom felt like the worst husband ever when it came to answering the officer's questions. What was Brenda wearing? What did she have with her? Where would she go? After forty-plus years of marriage, Tom suddenly felt like a very inadequate contestant on the old television game show 'Mr and Mrs.' Fortunately, Brian and Julie helped fill in some of the blanks. The officer took down the details and asked for a recent photograph. He also asked Tom if he was happy for them to issue an appeal via the media. Tom said he was.

Just after 6 pm, Cheryl and the two boys appeared. Brian had called them, and they insisted that they wanted to come over and support Tom. Julie made some tea for the boys, and Brian went for another drive around. Cheryl sat in the living room with Tom.

Neither had anything to say. They sat in silence, staring into the middle distance.

As the hours passed, the mood in the house became more sombre. Cheryl and Julie put the kids to bed in Tom and Brenda's room.

The police officer returned around 10 pm with a couple of other colleagues and said they needed to eliminate a few things from their enquiries. They looked through each room in the house and then asked to see inside the garden shed and outbuildings. They also wanted to do the same at Brian and Julie's addresses. Brian and Julie duly returned home to let the police conduct their searches. They had no idea what they were looking for. Having strangers rummaging through drawers and cupboards was highly uncomfortable. Julie was beginning to feel guilty, and she had no idea why.

The gravity of the situation was now beginning to hit home. It was nearly midnight, and there was still no news of Brenda. She had been missing for nigh on 12 hours. Where on earth could she be? Tom was desperate. Brenda was the love of his life. His soul mate. He couldn't comprehend a future without her. All manner of awful scenarios were playing out in his head. Had she fallen from the cliffs or been kidnapped by some maniac? He began to think there could be no good outcome to the situation.

He made his excuses and went out into the garden. The air was cool but welcoming. It was a clear night, just the right kind for enjoying the garden. He sat on the bench at the bottom of the path. They had positioned it there to get a nice view of the rose trees. Brenda loved roses. Tom had never bought her any cut ones, he didn't believe in Valentine's Day, and for her birthday, he would much prefer to get her a plant for the garden than something that would only give pleasure for a week. Had he been a good enough husband? He certainly hadn't been perfect, that was for sure, far from it.

As a younger man, he had had his fair share of flings. He was that stereotype - a woman in every port. He loved his wife and family, but he never gave them a second thought when he was alone in a strange place. *That sounded callous.* He was pretty shocked himself with how easily he could compartmentalise his feelings.

He lived in the moment, and in those moments, he desired the company of a woman. It might have been lust that drove him into the arms of others, but he sought more than just sexual gratification. He liked the smell of a woman on his skin and the feel of their curves under his hand. He could love

79

them and leave them without any sense of remorse or guilt. *Did he feel guilty now? He rather thought he did.* Perhaps it was Brenda's illness that had stirred these new emotions.

If Brenda ever suspected anything over the years, she had never let on. When he was home from the sea, he was an attentive lover and devoted father. He could switch back into family mode as soon as his feet made terra firma. Did that make him an evil man? Tom knew full well that he hadn't stuck to the letter of his marriage vows, but at the same time, he didn't feel his actions overseas lessened his love for Brenda or his performance as a husband.

Had she found out, well, that would have been different entirely.

He had never stopped to consider the consequences of his actions.

Sitting now in the still of the night, Tom came face to face with reality for the first time. What if she had found out and had left him. His stomach growled. He hadn't eaten all day. He felt another wave of nausea. What if he never saw her again?

Dementia might be erasing the woman she was, but she was still his Brenda. There had been times recently, he was almost too ashamed to admit it, when he had wondered if she would be better off dead than suffering the journey that dementia had in store for her. Was he thinking of her or himself in those dark thoughts? The horror of the situation hit home. How would he cope if she was gone? He wasn't that keen on his own company. He liked people around him. Then there was Liz. Had she come back into his life for a reason? Tom snapped back into the here and now. He realised he had allowed his thoughts to drift. He was supposed to be thinking about Brenda, out there all alone, probably lost and frightened. This wasn't the time to be thinking of Liz ... or Christopher.

Brian and Julie were also out of rational reasons why the police hadn't yet found their mum. The pair were keeping quiet. Platitudes were no longer appropriate. Having suffered the indignity of having their homes searched and being made to feel like criminals, they sat in silence on the fading blue velour sofa, willing the phone to ring or the police to come back with some good news.

They must have drifted off because it was nearly 8 am when the phone did ring. The shrill sound made them startle. Tom's heart was beating so fast he felt it would jump out of his body.

"Hello," he said weakly. He wasn't sure if he wanted to hear what was coming next.

"Mr Beresford, this is DS Jones. I am pleased to say we have found your wife, and we are bringing her home now. We found her outside McKinley and Sons, and I gather she used to work there?"

"Yes, yes she did. Goodness, how on earth did she get there? Oh, thank you so much, thank you."

Tom replaced the receiver. He couldn't believe his precious wife was safe. He turned to the children.

"Your mum is safe. They found her outside McKinley and Sons, but I don't know any more than that. They are bringing her home now."

Tom couldn't keep his emotions in check any longer. He began to sob.

"Come on, dad, it's all over now. Mum's safe," reassured Julie putting her arm around him. Tom sank into her tender body.

"I'll go and tell the boys," said Cheryl heading upstairs. "They will be relieved. Archie has been awake most of the night, and he is exhausted."

*

There was a knock on the door. Tom bolted out of his chair. The plain-clothed detective stood there with Brenda by his side.

"Brenda, love, am I pleased to see you." Tom motioned forward to give her the biggest hug of her life, but he was stopped in his tracks.

"Who are you?" Brenda recoiled from his advances.

Tom's heart splintered into a million pieces. Not now. Not just when he needed her.

"It's alright, Brenda, this is your home, and this is your husband, Tom."

DS Jones ushered Brenda down the hall and into the living room. On seeing her son and daughter, Brenda's mood shifted.

"Hello, Brian, Julie, what are you doing here? Do you want a cup of tea?"

"Yes, please, mum, that would be lovely. Let me

give you a hand." Julie shot a knowing look to her dad and brother and accompanied her mum into the kitchen.

Brian sighed and slumped further into the sofa.

"Please have a seat, DS Jones. Thank you so much for finding Brenda. Do you know any more about where Brenda was for all those hours?"

"It seems she walked to McKinley and Sons and got talking to one of her old work colleagues, Kathleen Harrison?"

Tom looked vague. "That name doesn't ring any bells with me, but it was a large office she worked in, and she was the office manager, so I suppose she knew lots of people."

"Well, Mrs Harrison took her home. They had a good catch up about old times, and she had no idea that anything was amiss. They went back to Mrs Harrison's, had a meal and shared some wine, so she offered to let Brenda stay the night. It was only this morning that she realised something was wrong when Brenda wasn't making much sense. She talked about going into work, and when Mrs Harrison reminded her that she was retired, she refused to believe her. Mrs Harrison called the police, and we were able to go and collect her."

"So, whilst we were worried sick, Brenda was out enjoying herself!" Quipped Tom.

"If Brenda is going to be prone to wandering off, there are things you can put in place to help. Now she is on our system, it will flag her up if she does go missing again. I'll leave you with this leaflet that has some more information. I know right now all you want to do is relax with your wife."

"Thank you. We will have a read. I hope we never have to go through anything like this again, but I am sure it is best to prepare."

Tom showed DS Jones out.

All he wanted to do now was to hug Brenda and not let her out of his sight.

Chapter Ten

The days following Brenda's vanishing act were tense for everyone. Tom was wary of her every move, and Brian and Julie were more attentive than usual. Brian had 'popped' round a couple of times, and Julie had also put in an extra appearance. For her part, Brenda was blissfully unaware of the episode and slipped back into her usual routine.

When it got to Wednesday again, Tom wasn't sure whether to go to the cafe or not. Brian had reassured him several times that everything would be alright and he wouldn't make the same mistake twice, but that wasn't the only reason Tom was hesitant. He had not had a chance to digest the news from his last meeting with Liz with all the commotion. The earth-shattering news that he had a child somewhere out there had been left in abeyance, and only now did he have the mental capacity to go back to the issue and start to contemplate what it meant.

Did he want to make contact with his son, she had asked. What a question. He was in turmoil. Of course, a massive part of him said yes; he wanted to rush out and find his son. He wanted to know everything about him and be part of his life from this day forward. Then, the other part said, hang on a minute, you have a wife and family here that need you. What will it do to them if you suddenly announce that you have a new family? Then there was the other complication, what if his son didn't want to know them. How would that feel? There was no easy answer. It seemed someone would get hurt whichever decision he made.

In the end, Tom felt that he owed it to Liz to go to the cafe and see if she had any news.

He saw her sitting at 'their' table hugging a mug of tea. He ordered a drink and his customary slice of Bakewell Tart. As he drew near, she smiled, and he noted how beautiful she still looked. She carried a few more pounds than she did in her youth and had a few more lines, but all the same, she was beautiful. Her skin was clear, and her blue eyes were as sparkling as ever. He couldn't resist giving her a peck on the cheek as he took his place opposite her.

"Well, what a week." He sighed and gulped his coffee.

"How are things at home? I've been worrying about you all week," Liz said. Tom appreciated that she cared enough to worry.

"We are all OK now, but Brenda gave me the worst couple of days of my life last week.

"Last Wednesday, when I got home, she had disappeared, wandered out of the back gate. We had no idea where she was for nearly 24 hours, had the police involved and everything. We were worried sick."

"I can imagine what you must have gone through. I once lost sight of my daughter, Sarah, in a crowded shop when she was about two years old. We got separated, and for about ten minutes I couldn't find her. Talk about panic-stricken. I was beside myself. So Brenda going missing for 24 hours must have been unbearable."

"What happened?" Asked Tom.

"To Sarah, in the shop?"

"Oh, one of the security guards found her and put out an announcement over the tannoy for anyone who had lost a child to go the manager's office. I would never have forgiven myself if anything happened to her."

"Do you have help with Brenda, or is it just you?"

Tom swallowed his mouthful of cake and took a swig of tea.

"Most of the time, it is just me. I can cope with most things. Brenda has good days and bad. She doesn't know who I am on a bad day, and she can get upset if she thinks I am a stranger. Those are the times I struggle. Brian comes over once a week on a Wednesday to sit with her for an hour or two, which is why I can get away to the cafe. I started coming here as a way of recharging my batteries. It's nice to be able to switch off for a while and think about something else.

"Up until last week, she had never wandered off. If it becomes a regular thing, then I may have to think of getting some more help. She has been declining quite quickly, and I suppose I may have to consider a hospice or some form of a care home at some point before too long. Not a pleasant thought."

"Everything alright, Liz. Have I upset you?"

"I suppose it is just hearing you talk about your wife like that. I feel a bit awkward now, like I am 'the other woman.' I feel like we are cheating on Brenda."

"Well, we are only talking, aren't we? It's not like we are having a passionate affair."

"I guess not, but we do have a child together."

The mood had changed. Tom wasn't sure if he should call it a day or try to make amends. He seemed to have a knack for saying the wrong thing at the moment. He didn't set out to cause any upset to anyone, but it looked like he had put his foot in it with Liz.

"Have you thought any more about telling your daughter about Christopher?"

"I think my Sarah will be shocked, but I am sure after she has got used to the idea she will like having a big brother. What about your two?"

"I don't know. Given that we adopted them because we thought we couldn't have our own children, they would find it difficult. I just hope they don't feel I will love them any less."

"If they were youngsters, maybe that would be a worry, but they are both grown-ups, so you would like to think that wouldn't be an issue. I still haven't heard anything from the adoption people. How long shall we give it?"

"I'll do a bit of research myself and see if I can find out about private investigators. Maybe that will speed things up.

Do you want to meet here again at the same time next week for a catch-up?"

"Yes. It's a date."

"Is it?" Tom teased.

She had to admit that she had been wondering what their meetings were. She quite liked the idea of having a date with Tom. She couldn't deny that she found him attractive and comfortably familiar. After Frank had died, she had pondered the possibilities of meeting someone else. The thought of making small talk and getting to know someone from scratch had seemed rather unappealing. She missed the ease with which she and Frank had been able to converse. After a million years of marriage, you fall into your own shorthand. The other person instinctively knows what you are referring to, and 'thingy' and 'what's it' have as much meaning as the proper nouns. She missed having someone to curl up with on the sofa of an evening and someone to snuggle up to in bed. She had even gone as far as wondering what it would be like to go to bed with Tom. Not that she was getting ahead of herself and thinking that was the direction their relationship was heading. It was just that having made a baby with him on their first fumbling teenage foray into sex, she had wondered how it would be the second time around, given that both of them would be so much more experienced. Anyway, now she knew he had a wife that needed him; she banished such thoughts. She felt terrible enough meeting him in a cafe, so she certainly wouldn't be entertaining notions of anything more.

As they left the cafe, Tom turned to Liz and gave her his now expected kiss on the cheek.

"Are you sure you don't mind coming to the same place every week? Do you want me to come to your house for a change?" Asked Tom.

"No, it's fine. I like having an excuse to get out and stretch my legs. See you next week."

Chapter Eleven

"Brian, I have to see you. Today if at all possible. Can we meet?"

Brian stared at his desk as he answered the phone. It was Cath. He wanted to go and see her, and he couldn't think of anything he wanted more right now than to climb into bed with her and enjoy all that her lithe, welcoming body had to offer.

However, he was at work and right now was not an option. He looked at his diary. He had meetings all afternoon. How could he engineer his way to seeing her? He didn't want to 'work late' again as that excuse was wearing a bit thin at home. Even though Cheryl knew of his fling with Cath, it was over as far as she was concerned. Having agreed to go to the counselling sessions, he had resolved that he would end things with Cath. Brian didn't want to lose Cheryl and the boys, and he had told Cath that they couldn't go on like they were. He just hadn't spelt out to her what he wanted. In truth, he enjoyed what he had now. The best of both worlds. A family and a lover. He didn't relish the prospect of telling Cath that it was over, and now here she was asking to meet him. The last thing he wanted was to see her and walk away. They had something special, a chemistry that was hard to resist. Whenever he saw her, whether in the supermarket or a bar, he wanted her, there was no denying it.

"Mary," Brian called through the wall to his PA ",

can you move my 3 pm meeting with Derek Charlton to next week? I have a feeling the 2 pm with Roger Stephenson is going to be a long one. I'd be surprised if I get back to the office at all this afternoon. "

"Right you are, Brian. I'll give Derek's PA a call now to rearrange. Don't forget you have Archie's Parents' Evening tonight at school."

Mary was a good egg. She had been his secretary for the past ten years, and they worked well together. She was a hard worker and a formidable gatekeeper. She gave unwanted visitors sharp shrift if they thought they were going to interrupt Brian without an appointment. She fielded his phone calls and could always be relied upon to get him out of sticky situations. She had worked at the company for years and knew all the other PAs. She had worked with many of them in the typing pool when 20 of them were crammed into a windowless office furiously bashing out memos, letters and carbon copies. Mary would most likely know the answer if you wanted to know what was going on around the building. She would garner the gossip from the secretaries, mailroom and canteen, but Brian trusted her implicitly not to pass on anything that said between the two of them. As long as Mary got away promptly on a Friday to go to her Keep Fit class, there was nothing she wouldn't do for Brian. Brian felt bad about deceiving her, but he couldn't help it.

For her part, Mary wasn't quite as naive as Brian

painted her.

She knew all too well what he was up to, but he treated her well, and it wasn't any of her business if he chose to cheat on his wife, which is what she presumed he was doing. She had no evidence to back up her suspicion, and as long as that was the case, she consoled herself that she wasn't complicit in his wrongdoing. When his wife phoned the office, she could say with a clear conscience that he was in a meeting because it stated so in his diary.

"I can come round to yours about 3.30 pm. Is that OK? Great. See you soon."

Brian was distracted throughout his meeting with Roger Stephenson. Roger was one of his oldest clients. Usually, the two men would swap family anecdotes and discuss football, cricket, or motor racing before getting down to business, depending on the time of year. Today Brian couldn't be bothered with the small talk. He wanted to be out of the office as quickly as possible and into the arms of Cath. He refused the usual coffee when he walked into Roger's office and plopped a ring-bound report on his desk.

"Everything you need is in the report. Why don't I give you a chance to digest it, and then we can meet up again next week?"

Brian didn't even sit down, choosing instead to hover in the doorway. Roger could be in no doubt that he wasn't stopping. It worked.

"OK, matey." Roger picked up the report and

started to thumb through it. "We can discuss it over a pint at the golf club next week if you fancy it?"

"Sure, I'll get Mary to set something up. See you then." and with that, he left.

It took just 20 minutes to reach Cath's place. He knocked gently on the door and then let himself in. Cath had given him a key within a month of their meeting. She was single and lived alone in a quiet cul-de-sac just outside the town centre. They usually met there as it was relatively risk-free. Cath worked mornings at the local school and was usually home by mid-afternoon.

Whilst Brian couldn't always get away so promptly, they had enjoyed many an afternoon of passion when Brian's diary had him in all manner of business negotiations.

Cath was sitting on the sofa in the living room when he went in. He couldn't help noticing the stark contrast between the slightly Bohemian look of Cath's place and the pristine showroom-like quality of his front room. Brian couldn't deny a tinge of disappointment that she wasn't waiting for him upstairs. He enjoyed her company, and they had spent hours talking and getting to know one another, but Brian liked it best of all when he called around, and she only had one thing on her mind. Today it appeared she wanted to talk.

"Hey, love. Is everything OK?" Brian asked.

"Well, that depends. Sit down. Do you want a coffee?"

"No, I'm fine. What do you mean, it depends?"

"It depends on your point of view." Cath was somewhat cryptic. Brian didn't have time for games and was getting a little frustrated.

"Spit it out, Cath. What is it?"

"I'm pregnant." Of all the things he imagined that she would say, that was not one of them. They had always been careful and used protection. Even when they had got carried away that time in the car park, at the back of the theatre, Brian had been careful. He couldn't take this in.

"Are you sure?"

"Yes. I have been to the doctor's, and he confirmed it. I'm three months."

"Brighton," they said in unison.

Brian had been on a conference with work. Instead of staying in the same hotel as his colleagues, he had made excuses that it was full and he had found a cheap B&B close by. In truth, he had booked a double room at the Radisson for him and Cath. They had enjoyed three nights together, but he still thought he had been careful.

"How? I thought..."

"Just one of those things", Cath interrupted. "So, what do you think?"

"What do you mean, what do I think? I can't quite take this in. Why, what do you think?"

"I think it's wonderful. I want to have this baby. I am not putting any pressure on you to leave your wife, but I hope you will be part of its life."

Leave his wife? Cath had had time to think about this. Brian was reeling.

"When did you find out?"

"Last week. I couldn't tell you any sooner because I needed time to come to terms with things. I have always wanted a child, but I had imagined I would be married or at least in a long term relationship before I had one. I know this isn't the ideal situation, but I am happy to do this alone if I have to. I'm not getting any younger, and anyway, I'm thrilled. I just hope you are."

Thrilled was not the first adjective that came to Brian's mind. Could he face being a dad all over again? This changed everything. How could he go home and tell Cheryl that he had fathered a child to another woman? What would the boys say? What about his dad? He could have done with talking this through with his mother. She would know what he should do. Six months ago, that was exactly what he would have done.

"I'm sorry, Cath, you are going to have to give me a bit more time to get my head around this. I'll support you whatever happens. I just need time to think. Don't suppose you fancy going upstairs, do you?"

"Brian," Cath slapped his arm playfully. "Honestly, you never change."

*

As Brian pulled into the driveway at home, he still wasn't sure how to play things. Should he come clean to Cheryl, or was he committed to making a go of the marriage? Did he love Cath enough to leave his wife? The boys were of a great age now where they could have good times together, and he still loved Cheryl, despite all their ups and downs. Now, sitting here contemplating the thought of being a dad all over again, he couldn't deny the temptation of a clean slate. He could be there for this new baby in a way that he wasn't when Daniel and Archie were small. But then could he be enough of a dad to the baby anyway without giving up what he had at home? This was too big for him to consider now. He would have to sleep on it. He braced himself and went in.

A scene of domestic bliss greeted him. Cheryl was in the kitchen. A tray of fresh biscuits were cooling on a rack on the island. Cheryl caught Brian's look.

"For Archie, for school tomorrow. He didn't tell me, of course, until we got all the way home that they had to take something in for a school party. It was easier to make these than go to the supermarket."

"They look good."

In the living room, the boys were sprawled on the sofa idly watching television.

"Dad, dad, come and watch this," encouraged Archie "this lion is chasing an antelope. I think he's going to eat it."

Brian smiled and squeezed himself between the two boys. Could he walk away from them?

Chapter Twelve

Cheryl enjoyed the sensation as the water from the shower cascaded down her slim body. These precious moments captured first thing in the morning were sacred. It was the one time in the day when she was truly alone. In a few minutes, she would be mum again, but for a few seconds more, she could be herself. As she shampooed her long, strawberry blond hair, she recalled last night's lovemaking. Brian had been unusually attentive, taking his time to make sure she had maximum enjoyment. There hadn't been much intimacy between them lately since she had found out about the affair, but she was determined that she would get things back on track. As far as she was concerned, his wandering was a wake-up call for her, and she had to make sure she gave him no more reasons to look anywhere else.

She couldn't pretend that she had not been shocked and hugely disappointed when she had first uncovered the truth about his affair. She had always taken pride in her appearance. She had ensured the weight gained during her pregnancies had been shifted within a few months and her running gave her a body that was as toned and supple as the day Brian met her. When she looked in the mirror, a youthful, vibrant woman looked back at her. He used to tell her she was beautiful - he had told her so last night - so why had he felt the need to turn to someone else?

Cheryl was adamant that she didn't want to know anything about Cath. If she had details, she would be forced to imagine the two of them together. This way, she was less real. A name but nothing more. She had hated the moment during their counselling session when Brian described how they had wined and dined together. That had made Cath more three dimensional. The last thing she needed was to picture them holding hands across a candle-lit restaurant. As far as she was concerned, Cath was insignificant. A blip.

Whilst she didn't want to make excuses for Brian, she did sort of understand. She was no stranger to temptation. At work, she had had her fair share of admirers, and there had been a very close encounter at the Christmas Party when one of the partners had got just a little too friendly. She could still remember the sensation to this day of his mouth getting within millimetres of hers. Her body had ached for him to kiss her, but she had managed to pull back just in time to rescue her conscience and her reputation. If she could resist, why couldn't he?

She loved him, though, more than anything. When she found Brian, she felt like she had come home. He made her feel safe. He was five years older and seemed infinitely wiser. Unlike her, he had been to university and was now well established in his job at the architect's office. She had rejected further education choosing instead to start earning as soon as she could. She had not found her niche, though and had tried a string of jobs, none of which she enjoyed. When they met, she was working as a receptionist for a firm of accountants. Brian had been a client. They talked and flirted as he waited in reception waiting to go in for his appointment or on the way out when he used to ask her to book him a taxi. He wooed her with flowers and chocolates. Beautiful bouquets would be delivered to her work, making all the other women in the building envy her. She loved him for those grand gestures. They made her feel special, and she loved the attention they drew from all around her.

They had married shortly after, and within the year Daniel was born. She had relished being a mother, and when Archie arrived two years later, their family was complete. Brian was a doting father, and they soon settled into the perfect routine. She had stayed at home until Daniel was about to move to junior school, and Archie was settled in primary school. Only then could she face leaving them. She had managed to return to her previous role and had enjoyed having a reason to dress up again, swapping the comfort of mummy clothes for the tailored suits and killer heels that were her signature office wear.

Speaking to her girlfriends over a glass of Prosecco or three one evening shortly after finding out about Brian's infidelity, they had argued for her walking away and setting up on her own. "I

would never forgive Mark if he did that to me",
Bethany had said, and they had all chimed in
agreement. "You should take the kids and go."

"Go where?" Cheryl could not contemplate the
thought of leaving the family home that she had so
painstakingly created. She had agonised over
every inch of the wallpaper, curtains and carpets.
She had created mood boards and carried around
fabric samples for months until she was satisfied
she had just the right shade of ecru for the living
room. No, she wasn't going anywhere and any
way, how would she cope? The girls seemed to be
giving her far too much credit.

"You are strong, and you don't need a man to
define you. The boys are at a good age. Show him
who the boss is." Was it just the booze talking, or
would they be quite so self-assured about taking
their own advice?

Cheryl didn't feel strong. She had learned to put
on a brave face. She had had to. When her sister
had been killed in a motorbike accident at just
turned eighteen, Cheryl had lost everything she
cared about. There was barely a year in age
difference between her and Megan, and as
children, they had often pretended they were
twins. They dressed alike and thought alike. Just
like twins, when one hurt, the other one cried.
When Megan died, Cheryl truly believed a part of
her had died with her. The loss had destroyed her
parents. They were overwhelmed by grief and had
become virtual hermits. For the first few years,

Cheryl was the same, lost in a spiral of grief and depression.

She stopped going out. Her friends lost interest in her, and her world consisted of the four walls of her bedroom.

As a bright student, her parents expected her to go to university and follow in her sister's footsteps, but Cheryl could no longer consider university once Megan died. That is where Megan would have excelled. She had been talking of university from an early age, and she dreamed of the vast lecture halls and staying up until the early hours discussing some esoteric literature with like-minded peers. She had watched University Challenge religiously, seeing herself on the panel beaming back to her adoring family at home.

Eventually, Cheryl had emerged from the cocoon of her despair. She needed to earn a living. Her parents barely survived, and Cheryl needed to lead the way back to some sense of normalcy. She had forced herself to put on her war paint, her mask of confidence and get back to work. She had changed, though. She had put up an invisible shield. She didn't let anyone get too close. If they couldn't love her, they couldn't hurt her. She couldn't bear the thought of losing anyone else she loved, so she didn't let anyone get close enough. Only Brian had managed to penetrate her defences.

He had helped her to build her confidence. He had showered her with compliments and praised her endeavours. He told anyone that would listen about her many accomplishments as a wife, mother and homemaker. He was proud of her. Gradually she found her feet. Then the discovery of the affair had knocked her for six. She had allowed herself to entertain all her doubts and insecurities all over again. The nagging voice in her head was telling her she wasn't worthy of a man like Brian and that it was all her fault that he had strayed. Right now, she didn't feel confident. She could not imagine life on her own, raising the boys as a single parent. Instead, she clung to the idea that she could turn things around. She could show Brian that she and the boys were everything he needed. She would work at being a better wife and mother and ensure that she kept her man satisfied.

Losing him was not an option, and that was when she had suggested marriage counselling.

Cheryl had been surprised and delighted when Brian had agreed to go. She had thought he would find it too 'touchy-feely.' He wasn't one for talking about feelings, but he seemed genuinely remorseful about the affair and willing to do whatever it took to reassure her that he was committed to the marriage.

Chapter Thirteen

"Tea or coffee, mum?" asked Sarah, switching the kettle on and grabbing two mugs from the draining board.

"Coffee, please, love. Busy day?"

It was the usual question. Sarah couldn't remember the last time she hadn't been busy. It had been a good six months since they had last been on holiday, and what with work, the kids and in-laws, her life seemed one constant stream of busyness.

She helped herself to a couple of biscuits from the tin while waiting for the kettle to boil. It would be late by the time she got home and cooked tea, so she needed something to keep her going.

"I got you some of that cheese you like from the supermarket. I've put it in the fridge."

"Oh, thanks, love. That was kind. Here come and sit down." Sarah sank into the comfort of the large, beige sofa. Almost immediately, her eyes closed.

"You look shattered, love. Have you been overdoing it again?"

Blinking awake, Sarah smiled at her mum "no more than usual. We've been fairly busy at work, and the girls have had a full-on weekend. Amelia went to York on Saturday to go shopping with a friend, so I drove her over there, and then Becca had a swimming gala on Sunday. I hardly had time to flick a duster or put the Hoover on. It's a good job I haven't got visitors."

"You are too hard on yourself, love. Your place is always spotless. I'll tell you what you could do with, a few days away. Why don't you go and have one of those massages you like. If you pass me that magazine on the coffee table, I saw an article in there for somewhere that looked right up your street."

As Sarah moved towards the coffee table, Liz suddenly noticed the opened envelope just underneath the magazine. Too late.

Before she had time to do anything about it, Sarah was reading the contents. There in black and white for all to see was Liz's life laid bare.

"We are pleased to inform you that Christopher John Hargreaves is on our register and has indicated that he does wish to be contacted by his birth parents. To this end, we have forwarded your contact details."

"Mum, what's this all about? Who is Christopher John Hargreaves?" As Sarah got to the end of the question, Liz could see that she had already worked it out.

"Hargreaves was your maiden name. Mum, is Christopher your son?" Suddenly Sarah froze. Her face contorted with pain. Liz had never seen such a look on her face.

"Yes. Oh, Sarah. I'm sorry you had to find out like this. I never expected in a million years that I would find Christopher, let alone that he would want to be found."

Sarah made her way back to the sofa. She couldn't believe what she had just read.

Liz had only received the letter that morning. She had never dared to believe she would get the news she wanted. Now, not only did she know that Christopher was a) alive and b) interested in finding his birth parents, but she had to deal with Sarah finding out. She had hoped she might have been able to process the Christopher side of things on her own for the time being.

She owed it to Sarah to explain.

"So, Christopher", Sarah ventured.

"I might as well start at the beginning. I got pregnant when I was 17, nearly 18. I was due to go to London to start my training to become a nurse. My parents arranged for me to stay with an auntie until the birth. You have to remember they were very different times back in the late 1940s. There was no way I could have a baby as a young single mother, so I put him up for adoption. Of course, there hasn't been a day go by when I haven't thought about him, but I have never made any attempt to find him until now."

Sarah needed some space.

"I'll make us another drink." She needed to get out of the room. Sarah leaned on the kitchen worktop, her head bowed. Thoughts raced through her head. Who was this woman who was masquerading as her mother? This harlot had got pregnant at 17. Sarah imagined the scenario if she had come home at 17 and shared that news with

Liz. All hell would have broken loose. She hadn't been best pleased when Sarah had told her she was getting married.

What a hypocrite. As she filled the kettle, Sarah wondered how her mum had managed to put on such a creative act. She deserved an Oscar for her performance. All these years of pretending to be the doting mother and loyal wife, and all along, she had a dirty little secret. How little she did, in fact, know her mother.

When she returned from the kitchen, Sarah put a tray on the coffee table in front of Liz. As well as the two mugs of tea, there was a plate of biscuits.

"Thought you might need some sugar for the shock."

Nice try, thought Liz, but Sarah didn't need an excuse to eat biscuits. She took after her. Neither of them could resist temptation. They ate when they were sad, when they were happy, and anywhere in between. They both carried excess weight, but they were too keen on the good things in life to consider going without. So, for the most part, they accepted their growing waistlines and consoled themselves with the thought that the diet could start next week.

"I can't believe you have never felt like talking about it before now. That is a hell of a secret to keep. Did dad know?"

"No. I didn't think there was anything to gain by telling him."

"And where does that leave me?" Sarah's usual

smile had vanished. She looked like a petulant child.

"What do you mean, where does it leave you? Apart from the fact that you have a brother you didn't know about, why should this change anything?"

"Of course, it changes things, and it means you have been lying to me my whole life. So who was the father? Do you know?"

"Sarah," snapped Liz, hurt. "That's an awful thing to say. Of course, I know. How could you say such a hurtful thing? I am not proud that I got pregnant so young, but unfortunately, it was the only time I had had sex. His name is Tom, and we were at school together, and we were very much in love."

"So, did he know about the baby?"

Sarah's probing was getting very uncomfortable, but Liz felt obliged to be as honest as she could be. Having kept the secret for so long, it was rather a relief in one way to be open about things.

"He didn't know until just recently. I know you will find this hard to believe, but I bumped into him quite by chance in a cafe down the road a few weeks ago, and I've been to see him a couple of times. Naturally, he was as shocked as you are now."

"Hold on a minute. This is like a storyline in a soap opera. You met Tom recently, and you've been sneaking around meeting up for coffee."

"I haven't been sneaking around. I might not have

told you, but I am single and free to have coffee with anyone I wish. There is no need to take that tone with me. If you are going to be unreasonable, perhaps we should change the subject."

"Sorry. I didn't mean that. It's just that finding out you have had another child is hard enough, but having the father on the scene also is a lot to take in. So how did Tom take it?"

"Well, now he has had time to come to terms with the news, he is thrilled. He thought he could not father children, and he and his wife had adopted their two, so it was rather poignant. His wife has dementia. He says he would be interested in meeting Christopher if it was a possibility."

"So what was it like meeting Tom after all those years? Do you still have feelings for him?"

"I suppose I am bound to have some feelings given that we had a child together. He seems as charming as ever, but as I said, he is married. You certainly don't have to worry about me finding a new husband."

"That's as maybe, but I have still got to get my head around the fact that I have a half-brother out there, and you are seeing an old flame. Any more secrets you want to share?"

"Oh Sarah, don't be like that. You know the last thing I want to do is hurt you, and I didn't set out to keep secrets from you.

Meeting Tom has been somewhat overwhelming, and I hadn't purposely not told you about him. I suppose I was just getting used to the idea of him being around before I shared the news. I think we should call it a day for now. I'm rather tired and would just like to be on my own."

"OK. I can take a hint. I need to be getting back anyway, or the girls will be passing out. Tea is going to be late enough as it is. See you when I bring the girls at the weekend?"

"Yes. I look forward to seeing you then."

Later that night, in the comfort of her bed, Liz tried to make sense of what had just happened. Was she about to make contact with her baby boy? She had endured so many years of heartache and pain, missing him every second of the day. She was not there for his birthdays and at Christmas. All the milestones she had not witnessed, starting school, getting a job, getting married, having children? Was he married? Did he even have children? So many questions. But what if they met and he didn't like her?

Perhaps he would be bitter about the way she had abandoned him. Liz couldn't bear the thought that he hated her. It was wonderful to think that they might meet, but she must caution herself against expecting too much. After all, right now, they were strangers.

Chapter Fourteen

"Will you come with me to my first scan?" Cath had asked yesterday evening. Brian had been trying to decide what to do ever since. There was a baby, and if he went along on Thursday, he would be able to see it.

Despite hours of contemplation, he had not been able to come up with a clear description of how he was feeling. It would have been so much easier if Cath wasn't so adamant about having the baby. Or would it? Could he condone getting rid of his flesh and blood? Well, she had made it clear that wasn't an option. So how would he play this now? He would have to come clean to Cheryl at some point. He would go to the scan and then decide.

"Are you alright, love? You look tired. Is something bothering you at work?" Cheryl watched Brian through the crack in the door to the en suite as he shaved and wondered what had kept him awake most of the night. She had felt him moving in the bed but didn't say anything in case Cath was on his mind. If only she knew how right she was.

"Yes, we are working on a big project. I might not be able to make it to the counselling session this week. I'll probably end up going to London. You could still go, though."

"Well, that didn't last long. The second session and you are finding excuses not to go," Cheryl snapped.

"I'm not making an excuse. It's just the way it is. You know I would go if I could." Brian hated himself for telling lies, but what could he do?

Cheryl pulled herself out of bed and slipped on her dressing gown, tying the belt into a knot with exaggerated enthusiasm. How dare he give up now just as the gory details of the affair had been opened up for her examination? She probably would still go on her own to the session, but that wasn't the point. She needed him to be there to hear how she was feeling and to hear what his dalliance had done to her. She wanted him to listen to what she had to say and not be able to tune out the way he did at home. Leaving him to finish up in the bathroom, Cheryl went to wake the boys.

"Archie, don't put too much milk on your cereal. How many times do I have to tell you? Daniel, can you please put that down and come and get your breakfast."

"Don't take it out on the kids", Brian uttered sotto voce "it's not their fault."

Cheryl could have screamed. She was seething with anger. How dare he talk to her like that, making out that she was in the wrong? She tried to ignore him.

"What time will you be home tonight?" She asked. "I shouldn't be late, about 6ish. What's for tea?"

"Shepherd's pie. If you are home first, can you put it in the oven?"

"Of course, are you picking the boys up from football then?"

"I usually do. Boys, come on, we are going to be late. Go and brush your teeth and get your coats on."

*

Cheryl had meant to go to the counselling session, but she had another idea when Thursday morning came around. After dropping the boys at school, she decided to go into town. Brian had left early to catch the train to London and wouldn't be back till late. What she needed was some retail therapy. She parked in the multi-storey and took the lift down to the shops. When it came to shopping, Cheryl planned her attack with military precision.

She would start at the department store before working her way down the mall. She would have coffee at the far end and then make her way back to the car park via the shops on the first floor.

By the time she made it to the cafe, Cheryl was already well laden with bags. She had had a successful morning and had managed to find several outfits that would be perfect for their upcoming holiday. On the return leg, she would see if she could pick up some bits for the boys. After another couple of hours, she was exhausted. She didn't like to think how much she had spent, but she knew it was too much. She would have to do her usual trick of hiding some of the shopping in the back of the wardrobe and fetching it out at a later date so that Brian wouldn't ask too many questions.

On leaving the multi-storey, she turned left onto the High Street. She passed a row of parked cars, including a silver BMW the same style as Brian's and pulling up at the traffic lights, she couldn't help but glance into the adjacent restaurant. For one awful moment, she thought she had seen Brian sitting at one of the tables. As the lights turned to green, she pulled away, but the man's image had etched onto her brain. Was it him? No, he was in London. It was impossible. Curiosity got the better of her, and she pulled over at the first opportunity.

Getting out of the car, Cheryl walked back towards the restaurant, her heart racing. As she got closer, she realised she didn't have a plan. Would she go in and confront him or just peer through the window?

Standing outside the restaurant, she pretended to be looking at the menu posted in a glass frame to the left of the entrance. She could see the man quite clearly now, and it was Brian. He was smiling and holding hands across the table with a woman. Cheryl couldn't see the woman's features, just the folds of a skirt showing below the table and some sparkly sandals. Anger, disappointment, disgust, she wasn't sure what she was feeling, but big, hot, salty tears were streaming down her face. She wiped frantically at her eyes with the sleeve of her jacket. She had to move. She didn't want anyone to see her, let alone Brian. Cheryl hurried back towards her car but stopped before reaching it. She had spotted a supermarket and made a last-minute decision to go in. In a blur of tears and gut-wrenching agony, she bought two bottles of wine and some sweets. Then she went back to her car. She sat for a few minutes to regain some composure and checked her make-up in the mirror of her compact. She looked like the proverbial panda. She did her best to make herself look presentable, but she couldn't conceal her puffy eyes. It was a good job that the boys were too young and too preoccupied to take much notice of her, she thought.

She was right. When she picked up the boys from their after school club, they were oblivious to her emotional state.

The conversation quickly turned to homework and football. With their dad 'away' for the evening, she had always intended to let them have a pizza in their rooms rather than sitting at the table for their usual family meal. She served up the tea, gave them each a packet of the sweets she had picked up earlier, and they disappeared into their respective lairs. Cheryl gave the kitchen a cursory wipe and then gathered up a large glass and one of the bottles of wine. She, too, needed to retreat to the comfort of her own space.

It wasn't long before the wine had taken its toll, and she fell asleep, still fully dressed, and spread-eagled across the king-size bed.

*

Waking to the sound of the alarm clock the following day, Cheryl very much regretted having finished the whole bottle of wine.

She was a bit of a lightweight when it came to alcohol, and apart from the very occasional night out with the girls, she wouldn't typically consume more than a celebratory glass of Prosecco. She reached for some Paracetamol. Standing in the shower moments later, the image of what she had seen came back to haunt her.

What was she going to do? Should she confront Brian or wait and see how much rope he needed to hang himself? London indeed.

*

Finally, the boys were in bed, and it was just her and Brian in the living room. Cheryl couldn't resist asking, "How was London? Did you manage to sort out the issues you were having?" She waited for the lies to begin.

"I never went to London. I'm sorry I lied, but I had to be somewhere else."

"Go on then. Where was this somewhere else?"

"Hospital."

Cheryl looked perplexed. She was taken aback that he had been honest enough to own up that he hadn't been to London, but what did he mean hospital?

"Looked more like a restaurant from where I was standing." She snapped.

"So you knew all along that I didn't go to London? Were you following me?"

"No, I just happened to see your car at the side of the road in town yesterday, and then I saw you sitting in the restaurant on the opposite side of the road when I was waiting at the traffic lights. I just wanted to see what lies you were going to tell me this time. I suppose you were with her, were you, Cath?"

"I'm sorry, this is hard. Cath's pregnant. It was her first scan at the hospital yesterday, and she asked me to go with her. I wasn't sure at first if I would, that's why I said I was going to London. I needed time to work out what I was going to do. In the end, I did go, and then we went to the restaurant. We were both rather emotional, and we needed to talk about what happens next."

"And, have you decided what is going to happen next?"

"Yes. I'm sorry, Cheryl, I'm leaving you. I have to be with Cath and the new baby."

Brian could see Cheryl physically recoil as though she punched in the chest. He hated the thought of hurting her, but this was a lose-lose situation, whichever way he thought about it.

"But what about the boys? They need you. You can't do that to them."

"I'll still be there for the boys. I know it won't be

easy, but plenty of families go through this sort of thing."

"So are you going to tell them then? They are going to be heartbroken."

"I think this is something we need to do together. Perhaps we can sit down with the boys at the weekend and explain."

"So what happens in the meantime, am I supposed to act like nothing has happened and try and play happy families?"

"I know I've hurt you, and I am sorry Cheryl, but for the sake of the boys, it would help if we could keep things as civilised as possible."

"And what about your mum and dad, do they know?"

"Not yet. I'll tell dad when I see him. It doesn't have to affect your relationship with them."

Beginning to feel nauseous, Cheryl had to leave the room. She ran down the hall to their bedroom and slammed the door behind her. She flung herself onto the bed and buried her head in the big, white fluffy pillows. She sobbed uncontrollably until finally, exhausted, she fell asleep.

Chapter Fifteen

Christopher grabbed his jacket and car keys and headed out of the house. The sky was overcast, and the air felt unseasonably cold; the ominous clouds overhead reflected his mood. He wasn't having a good month. He had missed his sales target and was in danger of missing out on his bonus. God knows he certainly needed it. As he turned the ignition, the CD stirred into life. Twenty minutes later, he was suitably psyched to face the office and the competition.

As he entered the office building, he breezed by two young women standing in the reception area.

"Morning, ladies."

"Did he just wink at us?"

"Probably. That's Christopher James from Sales. Total letch. Kim in Accounts said he patted her on the bum last week. I tell you, if that had been me, I would have been straight into HR to report him. He thinks he's God's gift to women."

"I know what you mean, but he is kind of cute!"

"Oh, not you as well. Half the women in the building think he is drop-dead gorgeous, but I don't see it myself. His eyes are too close together."

At his desk, Christopher surveyed the mountain of paperwork surrounding him. He was trying to ignore the unopened envelopes, just like he did at home when he spotted a far more interesting one from the Adoption Contact Register. It seemed his birth parents were ready and willing to make contact. The news made him stop in his tracks. After all these years, it might finally happen. He might get to meet the parents that not only made him but abandoned him.

"Coffee, Chris?" His PA, Pamela, stood at the doorway holding a number of mugs.

"Yes, please, Pam. Hey, you never guess what? I've heard back from the adoption people. My birth parents want to make contact."

"Oh wow. That's amazing. So what are you going to do? Are you going to see them?"

"That's the plan. Just got to work out when and where. Going to be bloody weird, though. What if I don't like them?"

"Or they don't like you", volunteered Pam.

"Nah, how could they not like a good looking bloke like me?"

"And so modest."

Pam disappeared and returned a few moments later with the coffee.

"Seriously though, Chris, are you sure you can handle meeting them. How do you feel about them?

"Well, I'm past being angry. I would like to know why they put me up for adoption, but I think I would like to get to know them if there is a chance of doing so. You just never know what you are going to find, and I might have brothers and sisters out there I never knew about."

"Let me know when you are going to meet them. I can help you rehearse if you want."

"It's not an interview. What are you trying to say, Pam?"

"Just that you can be a bit, you know, a bit full-on."

"Oh, you cheeky mare. Get out of here. Go and do some typing or whatever it is you do around here."

Pam went back to her desk. She was one of the few people who could talk bluntly to Chris. She had worked for him for just over two years. When she had first joined the company, the other PAs had tried to warn her off. He had a poor reputation among the women. According to the office gossip, he was a male chauvinist and a creep. She was determined not to pre-judge him and to find out for herself what made him tick. It was true he was full of macho bravado on the outside, mainly when he was in the vicinity of the other salesmen on the floor, but she quickly saw a softer side to his nature. Get him talking one to one, and you could see he was not as cocky as the others would have you believe. He had worked hard to get to where he was, and he was keen to do well. It was true he could be overbearing and self- centred, but as far as Pam was concerned, the bravado was because he felt he had to prove himself.

He had told her about being adopted, and she had seen a different side to him in those moments. She just hoped that if he did meet up with his birth parents, it wouldn't set him back. Hopefully, they would get to see the real him and passed the shallow, pushy salesman caricature that most of her colleagues saw. Christopher had to admit that whilst he was keen to be introduced to his parents, he was more nervous about that meeting than any sales pitch he had ever had to make. Hopefully, they would be suitably impressed by his executive car, designer clothes and minimalist bachelor pad, and they would see that he had made something of himself.

The agency had suggested that meeting both parents was too much too soon, and they recommended that Christopher start by simply meeting with his birth mother. And so, a couple of weeks later, the date was set. They agreed to meet at a service station on the M1. Quite how they would recognise each other, Christopher wasn't sure.

*

"Not exactly private is it," Christopher said as he took his cup and put it down on the table across from Liz. They were lucky to find a couple of empty chairs amid the crowd of travellers.

He had had no trouble identifying Liz. He had first spotted her standing outside the cafe, fidgeting with her necklace and carefully scrutinising each face that passed by to see if there was a glimmer of recognition. He had picked her out before he went into the newsagents to pick up a packet of mints and half a dozen scratchcards. He watched as she finally joined the queue and bought a drink. She looked as nervous as he felt.

So this was his mother, a plump, middle-aged woman with a mass of thick brown hair and stunning bright blue eyes. She looked smart - had she made an effort just for him? Her face was warm and friendly. She looked like someone who would listen to your woes and then give you a big hug.

"Never mind all that come here. Can I hug you?" Liz was standing up now, her arms out expectantly. Her heart was beating so fast she was sure he would feel it when he pressed against her. She felt clammy. She could feel beads of sweat forming at her brow. She wondered if her voice gave away the butterflies in her stomach.

"Of course."

"I have dreamed of this day for the past 50 years. I have thought about you every day. Giving you up was the hardest thing I have ever had to do." Liz was holding him so tightly, Christopher wondered if the hug would ever end.

Sitting back down, the two looked at each other. Liz didn't wait for his reaction,

"I was just 17 when I had you. The minute you were born, the midwife took you away, which was the last I saw of you. I hope you can understand?"

The words were pouring out of her like water cascading over a high waterfall. Too much too soon, she wondered? She couldn't help herself. Here he was now in front of her, a strapping hulk of a man. Her son. She still couldn't quite believe it, and all she wanted now was for him to know how very sorry she was that she hadn't been able to be there for him. Be the mother she had always longed to be. She caught her breath and stared into his intense dark brown eyes.

"It's not easy knowing you were some mistake that someone gave away."

"Oh, Christopher, love. Please don't say it like that. I might have been young, but I was very much in love with your father. We would have kept you and brought you up as part of our little family if we had had any say in the matter. I certainly never thought of you as a mistake. You were my beautiful baby boy who was wrenched from me. I have always loved you even though I have never been able to show it."

Christopher took a mouthful of his coffee. He could see Liz was genuinely remorseful for the situation, but he couldn't pretend to be feeling something he wasn't.

"So what happened to my father, who you loved so much?"

"Well, funny, you should ask that. When I found out I was pregnant, I didn't say anything to Tom, that's your father's name, Tom. He saw me last when he waved me off as I boarded a bus to London at 18. Anyway, I have just moved to Hainsborough, and well, you wouldn't believe it, but a few weeks ago, we bumped into each other for the first time in fifty years."

"Whoa, what are the odds of that? So, does he know about me?

"Yes. I had kept you a secret far too long. I told Tom everything."

"What did he say?"

"He was shocked naturally, and I suppose upset that he had missed out on having a son all these years. He and his wife couldn't have children, so they adopted a girl and a boy.

Knowing he had a biological son was a massive shock but also the most wonderful news. He would love to meet you. His wife has dementia, unfortunately, so he isn't having the easiest of times."

"What about you? Do you have a husband and children?"

"I was married. Frank died just over a year ago. I have a daughter, Sarah, and she has two young girls. I am sure this is an awful lot for you to deal with in one go, but I hope you will be able to meet them and feel more like part of the family in time. And you? Do you have a family?"

"I did. It didn't work out. We divorced just over five years ago. I have a daughter, Amy. She's 16, but I don't see much of her. They live in London. Her mum married again."

"So tell me a bit more about your life. Did you have a good childhood? Have you been happy?"

"It started OK. Peter and Marjorie adopted me as

a baby, and as far as I can remember, I had a good childhood. Then Peter died when I was about ten, and that was hard. I think I took that quite badly because I started to have a few problems at school after that. I didn't settle for anything, and I left school at 16, not knowing what I wanted to do. Anyway, I got into sales, and I seem to have found my niche.

"Marjorie remarried, but I have never hit it off with Martin. I still see Marjorie, although she is getting on now and isn't so well I try and avoid Martin to save any upset."

"What about brothers and sisters?"

"None. Just me."

"Oh, Christopher, I don't like to think of you as an only child. I had always imagined you surrounded by lots of family."

"Don't worry about me. It has never bothered me, and I'm doing great. I have a nice house, a top of the range car, plenty of holidays and good mates, so I don't feel like I am missing anything."

"There's more to life than possessions, though. I hope you will come and meet the rest of the family?"

"Of course. Be good to meet Tom. See where I get my good looks from." Christopher gave Liz a playful wink.

"Here, take my card. Ring me on my mobile phone when you have sorted something out. I have things planned for the next couple of weekends, but I should be free towards the end of the month."

"Mobile phone? Oh, I say you must be doing well if you have one of those. Okay, son, it's been lovely to meet you after all these years finally. Can I see you again?"

"You bet. Perhaps you can come over to mine next time. I think we need somewhere a bit more private now you know I am not some deranged madman, don't you?"

Liz watched as the tall, dark-haired semi-stranger walked away. The encounter had been brief, but she must be grateful that he had wanted to meet her at all. What did he think of her? Was he disappointed? He hadn't given much away, and she couldn't be sure what he was thinking. For her part, she was bursting with pride and love. That handsome, middle-aged man was her son, and she had him back in her life, where he was meant to be, and there was another grandchild. Would she ever get to meet Amy, she wondered.

Back in his car Christopher grabbed a coin and frantically rubbed his way through the stack of scratchcards. Absolutely nothing. He threw the shredded remnants onto the passenger side foot-well and started the engine.

Chapter Sixteen

"So tell me all about it. I have been on tenterhooks since I knew you were going to meet with Christopher. How did it go? What is he like? What did you talk about?"

"Steady on Tom. I can't get a word in edgewise."

"Sorry, it's just that I am so excited to hear about Christopher."

"Well, he has your looks. He's tall and dark and, I dare say, handsome. Bit of middle-aged spread but then haven't we all! He didn't give much away about his feelings, but he does want to meet you. He gave me his card so you can set up a meeting towards the end of the month. He seems to be doing well for himself. He has one of those mobile phones. He's divorced. He has a daughter called Amy, 16, but she lives in London with her mum and stepdad. It sounds like he had a fairly happy childhood but no brothers or sisters. He left school at 16 and found he liked selling, so that's what he has made his career."

Tom listened intently to what Liz was saying. Ever since she had told him he had a son, he had been trying to picture him. Now he was a step closer to finding out for himself what he was like.

"How do you feel now you've met him?"

"I don't know how to describe it. I've imagined meeting him so many times over the years, and of course, the reality was nothing like what I had concocted. I knew he was mine the minute I saw his face, and I felt full to bursting with motherly love..."

"But? I sense there is a but?"

"Not a but exactly. It's hard to put my finger on it. I just sensed something wasn't quite right. Christopher seemed a bit preoccupied. After all, it's the first time I have seen him. I suspect I just need to get to know him better."

"Well, they always say you can't choose your family. There was never a guarantee that things would go smoothly, but from what you have said, I think it seems a very positive start."

"That is what they counsel you about at the Adoption Service. They warn you not to get your hopes up because things might not go as well as you expected. The meeting itself was fine, and he seemed genuinely pleased to see me, and it's just he seemed as if he had more on his mind."

"There are probably bits of all of us that others don't like, but it doesn't stop them loving you. I know my Brian can drive me mad at times, and we've certainly had our battles with Julie along the way, but I wouldn't swap them. What about your Sarah? I bet there are things about her that you don't care for?"

"Well, right now, it's the fact that she isn't speaking to me."

"Why is that?"

"She found out about Christopher, and she's jealous."

"What does she have to be jealous of?"

"She has got this silly notion that because Christopher is my first born that once I get to have him back in my life, I am not going to want to know her and the girls."

"Well, that's crazy."

"Tell me about it. I've tried talking to her, but she doesn't want to know at the moment. She is giving me the silent treatment."

"Does she know you have met Christopher?"

"No, but she knows about you, and that didn't go down well either."

"How come?"

"She seems to think we are having an affair rather than a cup of coffee!"

"Chance would be a fine thing."

"TOM!"

"Are you telling me the thought hasn't crossed your mind? If I was single, like you?"

Liz blushed. She thought about all the nights she had lain awake since Tom had come back into her life. The fantasies that she had concocted of midnight strolls and long embraces. Liz could feel the colour rising from her toes, a wave of heat encapsulating her body. She was too old now for hot flushes, but he certainly had a way of awakening feelings in her that had laid dormant for a long time.

"I think we should change the subject..."

"So, what are you going to do about Sarah?"

"Just wait. She will come round in her own time.

She always does. Frank used to be the same. If something didn't suit him, he could sulk for days."

"Maybe my Brenda has the right idea after all then. She was always more of a have a good row and clear the air type. We've had some right ding dongs over the years."

"How is she?"

"Honestly, I think she is declining. She seems to have more bad days than good at the moment, and her memory is deteriorating. I am not sure how much longer I am going to be able to cope with her at home."

"Do you think she will have to go into a home?"

"Yes, I think some sort of care home or hospice before too long. It's alright when she knows me, but she can get quite violent when she doesn't. She thinks I am going to hurt her, and it's terrifying. She looks at me like I am a total stranger. If she continues like that, I will have no option as I can't feed her or take her to the toilet or anything. It's not safe for either of us."

"What do your children think?"

"I think they understand. Brian has seen how she can be, and Julie is very practical about these things. She tends to take the emotion out of situations and weigh up the pros and cons. I'll be heartbroken when it comes to it, but I have to be realistic. I can't see the present situation continuing for much longer."

"So, getting back to Christopher then. When do you think you will ring him, and where are you going to meet him?"

"I am going to ring him as soon as I can, probably this evening, and I suppose I could always arrange to have a pint with him somewhere."

Chapter Seventeen

"Mummy, I can't find a clean shirt for school?"

"Daniel, help your brother find a clean shirt or give him one of yours." Cheryl looked in the mirror and gave an almost audible gasp when she saw the dark circles that had formed overnight under her eyes. Her skin was looking sallow as if she hadn't seen daylight in weeks. Thinking about it, she had missed several morning runs, and she had turned down more than one offer of a walk with her neighbour this week. They had developed a nice routine, Penny with her bloodhound Bert and Cheryl with the boys on their scooters. They walked to the park where the boys would do a circuit round the paths whilst the two adults chatted, and Bert was allowed off the leash to run free.

She hadn't felt like it, though, these last few days. Brian had told the boys that he was leaving, and their world had come crashing down. She doubted things would ever feel normal again. The past 48 hours had been intense, and nobody had got any sleep. Archie had ended up in her bed for two nights running, and Daniel was even more of a recluse than usual.

Doing the laundry had been the last thing on Cheryl's mind, and as she said the words, she had a sinking feeling that clean shirts would not be forthcoming.

"I haven't got a clean shirt either. Mum, what are we going to do?"

"It's not the end of the world, Daniel. Just put on the shirt you wore for school on Friday, and I'll put a load in this evening."

"Uggh, gross."

"Come on. It's not that bad. There are plenty of children in the world who would be grateful to have more than one shirt, let alone a clean one every day. Just think yourself lucky."

Daniel rolled his eyes. Here we go again. He thought the 'think yourself lucky' speech. It was trotted out at regular intervals when they didn't eat all their vegetables when they wanted fizzy pop or sweets, any time his parents couldn't be bothered to come up with another reason why they couldn't have a new video game or pair of trainers. Daniel was sick of hearing about all the other children in the world. Right now, he was more concerned about what the boys in the playground were going to do to him when they saw him in his crumpled shirt and his cheap supermarket plimsolls. God forbid that they should find out that his dad had left home as well, and then they would go to town on him.

A few minutes later, they had all managed to make it to the car. Cheryl blinked in the morning sunlight and slid on a pair of tortoiseshell rimmed sunglasses.

"Why are you wearing sunglasses at 8'o' clock in the morning, mum?" Asked Archie.

"I've got a bit of a headache, and the light seemed to be hurting my eyes."

"You mean you've got a hangover", added Daniel.

"Don't you be so cheeky, young man."

"Mum, is dad ever coming back?" Archie's face contorted, and he looked like he was going to start crying again. If it was possible to do so, Cheryl's heart broke into even smaller pieces. Her poor babies were suffering, and she couldn't make it better for them.

"We'll have to see Archie. Right now, he needs to be with Cath and help her get ready for her new baby, but he will always be your daddy, and he will always love you and want to see you. He might not live with us, but you will still be able to see him whenever you want."

It didn't seem much consolation, but it was the best Cheryl could offer. Dropping the boys off at school, she turned and made her way to work.

*

"Morning Cheryl, a heavy night, was it? Don't tell me you went mad and had two glasses of wine?"

"Just because you have hollow legs where alcohol is concerned. You shouldn't mock your elders."

Cheryl smiled at Lucy and reluctantly removed her sunglasses. The glare from the daylight pierced the back of her eyeballs, and she winced in discomfort. The glass atrium where their reception desk was located was an unforgiving environment at the best times, but it was unbearable with a hangover.

"I'm just popping to the ladies. I won't be a minute. Cover for me," said Cheryl.

Inside the calm sanctuary of the ladies' powder room, Cheryl bravely faced her reflection. Thankfully she didn't look as bad as she felt, but her complexion was less dewy and youthful than of late. She looked tired and sad. As she applied another layer of lipstick, Cheryl painted on her smile. She was paid to smile at the visitors and sound bright and breezy on the telephone. She felt like doing neither of these things, but she was a professional, and she would get through another day just like she had done all the previous ones. She wouldn't let the outside world or even the inner world of Frazier and McMahon know anything was wrong. As far as they were concerned, her life was as pristine as the houses on the pages of the magazine she kept on the reception desk to read in between the phone calls and the visitors. Taking a deep breath, she went back to the atrium.

The plush grey leather chairs were already filling up with bodies. There were men in crisp, tailored suits and women in towering heels, with scraped back hair and prominent cheekbones. Suddenly Cheryl felt very under-dressed and inadequate.

She hadn't paid much attention to what she was putting on this morning and had opted for a tried and trusted green dress. It had always fitted her nicely, and she teamed it with black heels. Instead of feeling the familiar comfort of the garment, she now felt shabby and slightly embarrassed. She took her place behind the reception desk next to Lucy.

Lucy was nearly ten years younger than Cheryl and always looked gorgeous. She still had her youthful pre-child figure and long flowing locks of golden hair. Lucy was the kind of person that would look good in a bin liner Cheryl had often mused, and today, of course, she was looking radiant and flawless.

"Good morning Frazier and McMahon. How can I direct your call?" and she was off. The rest of the morning passed in a haze of call answering and visitor badge writing. By lunchtime, Cheryl was desperate for some fresh air.

"Luce, I'm going to pop out for a walk. Do you want anything?"

"I wouldn't mind a bagel if you are going past that place on the corner near the traffic lights."

"Sure, salmon and cream cheese and a bottle of water?"

"I must be getting predictable. Thanks. I'll settle up when you get back.

"OK. I won't be long."

Outside Cheryl replaced the dark sunglasses and took in a few deep breaths of urban air. She picked up the bagel for Lucy and one for herself and made her way to the local park. Plonking herself on one of the wooden benches, Cheryl cast around the other bodies doing similar. They were an assortment of office dwellers, each wearing the familiar corporate uniform and looking different shades of being harassed. As she ate her sandwich and felt the warmth of the midday sun on her face, Cheryl was suddenly aware of someone approaching. She looked up to see Mike Atkinson, one of the young paralegals from the office.

"Do you mind if I join you?" He asked, pointing at the space next to her on the bench.

"No, help yourself." Cheryl didn't know him that well. He was someone who had stopped to talk to her a few times as he passed through reception. He was of indeterminate age, with vivid green eyes and an engaging smile.

"I always like to get out of the office over lunch. If I don't get my fix of fresh air, I can't function in the afternoon. What about you?"

"Oh, I'm usually running around doing shopping at lunchtime, but I have a bit of a headache today, so I needed some air."

"Dare I ask, was the headache self-induced?"

"Why is it that everyone automatically thinks I have a hangover?" Cheryl replied in mock disdain.

"Maybe it says more about the person asking the question."

"Well, on this rare occasion, you are right, I'm sorry to say. I did happen to have one too many last night".

"I wouldn't usually be so bold, but I don't suppose you would consider joining me for the hair of the dog tonight, would you?"

Cheryl blushed. She was a married woman with two children. What was she doing getting chatted up by a young but rather good-looking work colleague? She was about to gracefully decline when her usually sensible inner voice went rogue for some unknown reason. If her husband could walk away and turn his affections elsewhere, why should she be the sensible one? So, instead of politely declining, she heard herself saying,

"I can't play out tonight, but if you fancy bringing a bottle around to mine, I can keep you company."

"OK. Sounds like a plan. Phone me when I am back at my desk with your address. "

"Just one thing though, Mike, let's keep this to ourselves. I don't want the likes of Lucy knowing the ins and outs of my private life.

"Sure. No worries. See you later."

Cheryl, what are you playing at? Almost as quickly as she had agreed to see him tonight, she was regretting her recklessness. Oh well, let's see if he turns up, thought Cheryl. Once he sees the house and the two kids, he'll probably run a mile, and there is nothing wrong with just having a drink with a work colleague, is there?

She knew she was kidding herself. What if it was Brian who had arranged to have a female colleague call round the house when she was away? Would she be so agreeable about the situation? All this made her head hurt even more.

*

It was a little after 9 pm when Cheryl opened the front door to Mike Atkinson. He had changed out of his officewear and had opted for jeans and a casual white shirt, which seemed to emphasise a tan that Cheryl hadn't noticed at work. She had to admit that he was handsome, and if pushed, she would also have to admit that she did find him attractive, sexy even.

For her part, she had made sure the boys were in bed by 8 pm with strict instructions not to leave their rooms, and she had showered and slipped on a summer dress. She hoped it gave the impression of something she would generally wear about the house, but the truth was she was more likely to be found wearing pyjama bottoms and a baggy t-shirt.

"Mike, you found me. Come in."

"This is not an area I know, but it looks pretty nice. Have you lived here long?

Cheryl took the two bottles of wine that Mike had brought and ushered him towards the living room. "Yes, we've been here about ten years now. It's a great area, and there are some great schools."

Mike smiled. Not the best topic of conversation, thought Cheryl, but then it wasn't like this was a date, and she was trying to impress him, was it?

"Have a seat, and I'll get some glasses."

Cheryl was surprised by how quickly the next three hours passed. The conversation had flowed effortlessly, and they had found several topics of mutual interest. They had polished off the two bottles that Mike had brought and started a third. Cheryl was now lying on the sofa with Mike on the floor in front of her, his head lolling against her legs. Any initial tension had disappeared, and they were now as comfortable as an old married couple. More so, if that old married couple were Cheryl and Brian.

Cheryl couldn't remember the last time she and Brian had shared such an intimate moment. She wondered for a second if Brian was enjoying a similar experience with Cath. Perhaps it was that very thought that prompted her next move.

It was heading for midnight, and Cheryl was conscious that she ought to be drawing things to a close. The only problem was that Mike was not picking up on her hints, and it was clear she would have to be more assertive.

"Mike, I've had a lovely evening, but I do need to be getting to bed. I don't normally drink on a school day."

"Lead the way", said Mike hedging his bets and to his great delight and even greater astonishment, Cheryl stood up, took his hand and led him towards her bedroom.

Chapter Eighteen

All too soon, it was 7 am, and the alarm clock on Cheryl's bedside table was ringing loudly. Turning to see the unfamiliar figure of Mike in the bed next to her, Cheryl's world turned to panic. How was she going to explain this to the boys? Had she just made the biggest mistake of her life or taken the first step towards a new one? It was too much too soon. Brian had only been gone a matter of weeks. The boys were still reeling from the break-up. It certainly wasn't the right time to be introducing them to someone new. How was she going to handle this?

"Mike, Mike, wake up. I need you to go into the spare room."

"What? What for?"

"I need it to look like you slept there last night and not in here with me. Quick nip next door before the boys wake up, please." Cheryl was pleading with him.

Reluctantly Mike got up and gathered his things. Hesitating, he turned and kissed her.

"Thanks for last night. I had a great time. I hope we can do this again? Can we talk later?"

"Sure, we can catch up at work but remember, not a word to anyone, particularly about you staying the night. This mustn't get out."

"OK. I'll let you get dressed and go downstairs, and then I'll come down."

*

"Boys, this is mummy's friend from work, Mike. He had a drink last night, so instead of driving home, he stayed in the spare room."

"Hi, Mike", chorused the boys and then paid him no more attention as they got on with eating their breakfast.

Cheryl steered Mike towards the door. Before turning the handle, he leaned in and gave her another kiss, this time on the lips. Cheryl felt her insides roll over. He certainly affected her, and whilst she had thoroughly enjoyed his company, she was also wracked with guilt.

On opening the door, Cheryl was shocked to see Julie and Zane walking up the path towards her.

"I'm guessing by the look on your face that you have forgotten that you said you would drop Zane off at school today and pick him up tonight?" Said Julie smiling.

"Sorry Julie, this is Mike. He's just leaving. Hello Zane, come in. The boys are waiting inside."

Mike smiled at Julie and made his way over to his car, turning to give Cheryl a wave before driving off.

"So how come you have a good looking chap leaving your house first thing in the morning?" Julie enquired innocently.

"Long story, tell you later," Cheryl whispered, indicating that she didn't want to talk about it in front of the children. Julie took the hint.

"OK. You can fill me in tonight when I pick Zane up. My conference finishes at 5 pm, so it will probably be around 6 pm by the time I get here."

"Stop for your tea, and then we can have a natter. I haven't seen you in ages and not since Brian left."

"Great. Thanks, Cheryl. We'd love to. Be good for your Auntie Cheryl Zane. Love you."

"Bye, mummy."

"Right then, boys, are we ready? Time we were heading off."

*

"Frasier and McMahon, how can I help you?"

"Is that Mrs Beresford? I am phoning from St Hilda's."

"Yes, it's Cheryl Beresford. Is something wrong?" Cheryl's heart was pounding. It was rarely good news when the school phoned. It usually meant one of the boys was sick.

"Mrs Beresford, this is Mrs Deakin, the headmistress. I'm afraid Daniel has been in a fight. Don't worry, he is not badly hurt, but I wonder if you would be able to come to school and collect him?"

"A fight? That's not like him. Of course. I'll come as soon as I can."

As Cheryl drove towards the school, her head was spinning with possibilities. She had never known Daniel to show any aggression. Perhaps he had been beaten up by bullies. Not badly hurt, what did that mean? He was hurt but not enough to warrant going to a hospital?

When she saw her son sitting in the Head's office, Cheryl could have wept. His young face was streaked with tears. His hair was sticky with sweat, and his shirt was ripped. On seeing Cheryl, he hung his head.

"Daniel, darling, are you alright? Are you hurt?" Trying his best to be brave, Daniel just shook his head.

"Daniel, why don't you wait outside in the office while I have a quick chat with your mummy?"

"Mrs Beresford, I have to ask, is everything alright at home?" Cheryl visibly stiffened at the question, but Mrs Deakin went on, "Daniel is such a lovely boy, and he never causes us any bother at all, but over the last few weeks, there has been a noticeable change in his behaviour. And I am not just talking about today's escapade."

An icy shiver ran down Cheryl's back. Had she noticed this change? Sure Daniel had been a bit more withdrawn at home, but he hadn't done anything to cause concern. As much as she didn't want other people knowing their business, she felt obliged to defend her son.

"Well, Daniel's father has left home. I thought he was coping with it, but perhaps I have been a bit naive."

"You ought to have told us, Mrs Beresford. These things can be very traumatic for a young boy, and if we know, we can look out for any changes and put things in place to help them cope."

Cheryl felt like she was ten years old all over again. She knew Mrs Deakin only had Daniel's best interest at heart, but her tone was enough to send Cheryl storming out of the office. She was not going to be lectured or given parenting advice by someone who had never even been married, let alone had a child of her own.

Cheryl grabbed Daniel and left.

Once outside, she turned to Daniel and gave him the biggest hug possible.

"Oh, Daniel, love. I'm so sorry. Let's get you home."

*

Having had tea, Cheryl had suggested to Julie that they put Zane to bed at hers along with the boys, so the two of them could have a good catch up. Cheryl poured them a large glass of wine, and they made their way through to the lounge.

"Poor old Daniel," said Cheryl, "as if he didn't have enough to cope with."

"Are you coping OK, Cheryl? I can't help noticing that the house isn't as pristine as normal. Daniel's having problems at school, and you had a rather early visitor. He just popped round for breakfast, had he? Is this all down to Brian leaving, the pig?"

"Oh, Julie. What have I done? I can't condemn Brian as I have just done something equally heinous?"

"What with breakfast, guy?" Julie was looking horrified.

Cheryl nodded.

"OK. Spill. Tell Auntie Julie all about it."

"It is so unlike me. You know how much I love Brian, and I would never normally dream of doing anything like this. I was devastated when he told me about Cath and the baby, and all I could do was think about how I could keep him here with the boys and me, and now I have gone and done something to drive him further away."

"Well, one step at a time. Just because you have screwed up, it doesn't follow that you have to tell Brian. So, how do you know lover boy?"

"From work. Mike is a genuinely nice guy, and I think he cares, but I never meant for this to happen. I had too much to drink, not that that is an excuse. I should never have asked him round, and he must have thought he was onto a good thing from the start.

"I was just flattered by the attention. When your husband leaves you for another woman, it is not exactly a vote of confidence. It did nothing for my self-esteem, and when Mike started showering me with compliments and paying me some attention, I just fell for it.

"I had planned just to have a drink with him, but foolishly I ended up sleeping with him. I'm so ashamed."

" I know how it happens. I'm certainly not going

to judge you. Look at me. I ended up with a kid and no bloke. There is no point in beating yourself up. It's happened now. The question is, do you want to carry on seeing him or was it a mistake?"

"Now is not the time for me to be seeing someone else. I've not been paying the boys enough attention, or else I would have seen what was going on with Daniel. I should be putting the boys first and trying to sort things out with Brian. And I need to stop pouring such big glasses of wine!"

"Why don't I have a word with dad and arrange for all of us to get together at his this weekend that way, you can have a good heart to heart with Brian. I am sure he is just as upset about things, and I know he loves you, and he must be missing the boys."

In the meantime, you go and put a wash on, and I'll have a bit of a tidy up.

"OK, thanks, Julie. You're a star."

Chapter Nineteen

"Daddy, daddy", shouted Archie running into Brian's arms as he walked over the threshold of Beechcroft Avenue.

"Hello, son. I've missed you. Where's Daniel?" Brian scooped Archie into his arms and planted a big kiss on his soft, warm cheek.

"We've missed you too, daddy. He's in the living room with granny and granddad. Daddy, are you coming home now?"

"It is not that simple, son, but you have to remember that just because I am not living at home with you, I still love you just as much. Let's go through and join the others."

As Brian pushed open the door to the living room, he was struck by how cosy the house looked with everyone in it. It reminded him of his childhood when the house always seemed full of people and laughter. His parents had always been good at throwing parties, and there never seemed to be a dull moment. The last time everyone had been together like this was for his dad's birthday. Today, the occasion wasn't so cheerful, but he liked the idea of them all being in the same place. He wasn't naive about how difficult the conversations were due to get, but he wanted to enjoy a few minutes of family time for now. Brian went around and kissed everyone on the cheek before taking his place next to Julie on the sofa.

Immediately he was rugby tackled by Daniel, who threw himself onto his lap.

"There's my lad. How are you doing, Daniel? I hear you've had a bit of bother at school?"

Daniel just shrugged and continued to bury his head into his father's jumper. Brian was overcome with a sense of love and parental protectiveness. He couldn't bear the thought of anyone hurting his son, and he hated the fact that he hadn't been there to kiss Daniel better when he had come home from school beaten up by the playground bullies.

"Right then, boys, why don't you go and have a kick about outside while us grownups have a natter", suggested Tom. The two boys dutifully left the room, much to their parents' surprise. It was as if they sensed the importance of what was to follow.

Brian couldn't help commenting, "blimey, not often they go without a fight. They are usually too scared of missing something."

"Now, I know we all have things we want to say to each other, and I am not sure if there is a right or wrong way of doing this, but while I have you all together, there is something I want to tell you," said Tom.

"God, dad, you are scaring me. You are not ill, are you?" Said, Julie

"No love. It's nothing like that. Suppose you let me say my bit. You know I have been going to the cafe each Wednesday, and a few weeks ago I met someone there who I hadn't seen in fifty years. Her name is Liz. Before seeing her in the cafe, the last time I saw her was when I waved her off on a bus as she left for London. She was just turned eighteen, and I was just that bit older.

"We went to the same school, and well, we were sweethearts. As far as I was concerned, if she hadn't broken up with me to go to London to train to be a nurse, we would have got married, and well, things would have been a bit different.

"Anyway, we have been getting to know each other again over the last few weeks, and she told me that when she went to London all those years ago, she was pregnant."

"Yours?" Julie asked, her eyes growing wider.

"Yes."

"After all the grief you gave me about having a kid without being married, and here you are fifty years earlier doing the self-same thing. You hypocrite."

"Hang on, Julie. I think you have just missed the point. I have only just found out about this. As far as I knew, I couldn't father children. Hence why you two were adopted. I know how it seems now, but this has all come as a massive shock."

"So, did she have the baby?"

"Yes. It turns out Liz had a boy called Christopher. He was put up for adoption as soon as he was born, and she hadn't seen him since. Well, until, that is, she traced him recently, and she met him for the first time last week. Now he wants to meet me."

"Are you going to meet him?"

"I would like to, very much, but that is why I am telling you now. I wanted to talk to you two about the situation. See how you feel."

"Whoa, dad. I knew I was coming here today for some heavy stuff, but I wasn't expecting this. So you have found out you have a son after fifty years, which means we have a stepbrother, and you want to know if we are OK with you meeting him?"

"In a nutshell."

There was silence. Nobody wanted to be the first to speak. Brian and Julie were trying to process what they had just heard, and Tom was desperately hoping they would find it in their hearts to be charitable. Being adopted themselves, would they feel more sympathetic about Christopher meeting up with his biological father, or would they feel rejected for the second time in their lives. He tried to anticipate their response, but their faces were blank like the very best poker players. Then after what seemed like an eternity.

"I don't have a problem with it, dad," said Brian. "I never planned on cheating on Cheryl and getting Cath pregnant. Now I have, I certainly want to be part of the child's life. I can't imagine having a child out there and not knowing them. When you do meet Christopher, do you plan on introducing him to the rest of us?

"I hope so. It depends on how it goes and if Christopher wants to get to know us. We'll have to take it a step at a time, but that would be ideal.

Julie, you're quiet. What do you think?"

"Well, like Brian, I suppose. Now you know you have a child, it would seem only natural that you want to meet them. I get that. I hope it does go well and that he does want to meet the rest of us."

"Great. I'm pleased you are both OK about this. I know it's a shock coming out of the blue like that, particularly when you are all facing your own problems. Why don't I go check on your mum and make another pot of tea?"

As Tom left the room, there was a perceptible sigh, like air escaping from a balloon. Brian stretched his arms above his head and exhaled loudly.

"Wow. I didn't see that one coming. Poor old dad. That must have been a bit of a shocker. So what do you reckon about this woman he's been seeing then? Do you think he still has the hots for her?"

"Oh Brian, you can be so uncouth at times." It was the first time Cheryl had spoken to him since he had arrived at his dad's house.

"What? It seems like a reasonable question."

"I am sure your dad has enough on his plate looking after your mum without thinking about another woman. I have found it difficult enough to find out about your love-child, so it must have been a heck of a shock to him after all these years. Just bumping into Liz must have been a big enough shock, let alone finding out about their child."

"Liz? How do you know her name?

"Because I listen to what is being said."

"Oh." Brian smiled nervously.

"Anyway, you two have a lot you need to discuss. Why don't I give you some privacy, and you can update Brian on what has happened at home and with Daniel. I'll go and give dad a hand with that tea."

"Thanks, Julie, appreciate it."

"So, what's has been going on at home then, Cheryl? Is everything OK?"

"Far from it. We have all missed you, Brian. The boys have been in bits since you left, and I haven't been coping that well."

"So, what's the story with Daniel fighting?"

"It's daft. He didn't have a clean shirt for school, so he had to go in one from the previous day. It shouldn't have been a big deal, but kids being kids, some thugs decided to pick on him for looking scruffy. They hit him, ripped his shirt. Oh, Brian, it was awful. You should have seen the expression on his face when I picked him up from school. He looked so small and sad." Tears were cascading down Cheryl's face.

Brian instinctively put his arm around his wife and pulled her close.

"Cheryl, I am so sorry I wasn't there for you. All of you. I have been so selfish. I love you and the boys. The last thing I meant to do was hurt you. I'm so confused about what to do for the best."

"Do you love Cath? Do you want to be with her?"

"I want to be there for the baby. I can't walk away from him or her, and I care about Cath, but if it is love, it doesn't stop me loving you and the boys."

"Well, you are going to have to decide, Brian. You can come home to the boys and me and still have a relationship with your other child, but you will have to choose. Do you want to be with Cath and see the boys at weekends or live with us and see your other child at weekends?"

Just then, there was a scream from the direction of the garden, and Brian jumped up and ran to the French doors.

"It's mum. She's fallen on the path."

Rushing outside, Brian found his mum prostrate on the floor, the two boys, ashen-faced, looking over her.

"Is granny dead?" Gasped Daniel

"No, darling, but she has banged her head on the floor and isn't feeling very well. You go inside to mummy and tell granddad to come out."

Tom came running outside from the kitchen. "Oh my God, Brenda, are you alright?"

"Dad, phone for an ambulance. Mum has bashed her head, and it looks rather nasty."

*

Two hours later, they were still sitting on the hard plastic chairs in the hospital's corridor. It took Julie to say something,

"Cheryl, why don't you take the boys home. They have been here long enough, and there is no point in us all hanging around. We can phone you as soon as there is any news."

"If you are sure. I suppose it has been a long day. Boys, hug your dad, and we'll go home."

"Are you not coming home with us tonight?" Asked Daniel, his tired eyes piercing Brian's very soul.

"I am going to wait here a bit longer and make sure granny is feeling better, but I'll see you very soon. I love you both. Be good for mummy."

Brian watched the two boys walk down the corridor away from him, clinging tightly to their mother. He felt sick for the pain he had caused.

Julie squeezed his arm, sensing his distress.

"They are such lovely lads, and they are missing you something rotten. You know Cheryl's been drinking, don't you?"

"What? No. She doesn't touch the stuff."

"Well, not normally perhaps, but since you left, she has been in a right state. You should have seen the house when I went round last week. It was a mess, and it didn't look like she had washed up or done any laundry for a month. There was no wonder Daniel didn't have a clean school shirt to wear."

"Why don't you try and make me feel even guiltier while you are at it" snapped Brian.

"Brian, I am not trying to make you feel guilty. I am just letting you know what has been happening. I understand you feel like you need to be with Cath, but you are married to Cheryl and have been for ten bloody years. She loves you. She has been distraught since you left. You do need to think long and hard about turning your back on them."

"I know. I can't do right for doing wrong. If I leave Cath, she will be in bits as well."

"Maybe, but it is a bit different for her. She knew you were married with a family when she got involved with you. She knew she was the other woman from the start. OK, so she is expecting your baby, but it doesn't give her an automatic right to you full time."

"So you think I should go back home to Cheryl and the kids?"

"Of course I do. You have a beautiful wife who adores you and two gorgeous kids who need you. It's a no-brainer ."

"When did you get to be so wise then?"

"About ten minutes after messing up my own life. Come here."

Julie threw her arms around Brian, and they held each other.

"So what do you reckon about this long lost stepbrother then?"

"Dunno. Be interesting to meet him. It will be weird for dad suddenly seeing his flesh and blood, and I just hope he still wants to know us when he sees his real kid."

"Don't be daft. Dad's not like that. Of course, he will still want us."

*

"Mr Beresford, can I have a word." The surgeon who had been operating on Brenda was standing in front of Tom.

"Brenda, is she alright?"

"It is too early to say I am afraid. Brenda has a lot of swelling in her brain. We have made her comfortable, and we are going to have to give this time. I suggest you all go home and have some sleep. We need to keep Brenda sedated for now."

"Can I see her, please? I haven't slept apart from her in what, five years?"

"Very well, but just you and only for a moment."

The surgeon led Tom into the ward. Brenda was barely recognisable. Her head was heavily bandaged, and it seemed like she had tubes coming out of every orifice. Tom winced. His poor darling wife. He leaned over and delicately planted a kiss on her forehead.

"I love you, Bren. Come back to me, you hear."

Chapter Twenty

Liz paced up and down her small sitting room picking up magazines and anything else left on the floor or the little brown table next to her favourite chair. Her daughter was upstairs refreshing her makeup, not that Liz could see anything wrong with it. Sarah had called round to her house a good hour before they were due to walk the short distance down to the café where they had arranged to meet Christopher. Liz was nervous about the meeting. The fact that Sarah was bothering about her appearance suggested to Liz that her daughter was too, although she was trying her best to pretend otherwise.

The first meeting with her son had passed in a bit of a blur for Liz, and she was hoping that she might feel a little more at ease this time. Right now, he was still a stranger, and it seemed there was an awful lot of small talk to be made before they could bond as a mother and son. She ached for the day when they would laugh and joke with each other and have that easy-going familiarity that comes with having a history of shared experiences. Would it ever be like that for them, she wondered? She had missed out on so much of his life and all the experiences that had shaped him and made him the man he was today. How different would he be if she had played the role she was meant to as his mother? Would he have turned out like his sister?

Liz always thought of her daughter as being a

159

fiercer version of herself. She had Liz's determined streak and, from an early age, had always been independent. Sarah was very much her own woman. She was head-strong, driven and career-focused. Sarah saw most things in black and white and would do anything to be correct. She had taken Liz by surprise when she had settled down and had a family as Liz never had her pegged as being the least bit maternal. As a child, Sarah was more interested in playing with cars than dolls. Throughout school and university, she had been determined to be the best at her chosen career, and there had been no mention of wanting children until she met Steve. When the children did come along, Sarah embraced motherhood with the same no-nonsense approach. She handled their day-to-day needs with a detached pragmatism, focusing on getting things done rather than worrying about their emotional well-being. It had fallen to Liz to give the girls the loving tenderness and human comfort they craved. It was a role Liz was only too happy to fulfil. She had more than enough love to go around and delighted in being able to snuggle up to her granddaughters and administer copious amounts of TLC.

Telling Sarah about Christopher had not been an easy thing to do. Sarah had always revelled in being an only child and had used it throughout her life as a bargaining chip to get all she could from her parents. It was true Liz had spoiled her. Hardly surprising, given that Liz had been overcompensating for the baby she had lost. Frank had chided Liz on many an occasion for pandering to their daughter's every desire. He worried that she had no comprehension of just how cosseted she had become. He did not need to worry, as it turned out, as, despite the overindulgence as a young girl, Sarah had worked hard for all that she had in adulthood. She had proved herself a hardworking and ambitious employee and an asset to the business. Now Sarah's position was being challenged. She was no longer an only child; she was now the younger child. She was feeling threatened by Christopher, and that was before they met. Liz had also sensed that she had gone down in Sarah's estimation. The thought of her mother getting pregnant at 17 and as a single woman had been a shock. Sarah was disappointed in Liz, and both of them were struggling to come to terms with this new way of seeing each other.

When Sarah finally appeared, Liz had to admit that her daughter was striking. Her brother couldn't fail to be impressed by this raven-haired beauty. She couldn't help but comment, "You look lovely, darling. Are you ready to meet your big brother?"

"Ready as I will ever be."

They walked the short distance down the hill in near silence, each rehearsing in their minds how the conversation ahead might unfold. Sarah had never been on a blind date, but she thought this was how it might feel as she approached the café with a mix of excitement and trepidation.

The café was a hive of activity. Most of the tables were occupied. There was a cacophony of voices competing with some indiscernible music being piped around the room. The woman behind the counter was engrossed in conversation with the man in front of her. From the way she was playing with her hair, Sarah concluded that she was enjoying his attention. For his part, he was smart and business-like, probably in his early fifties. He was leaning into the conversation and seemed oblivious to their presence.

"Sorry to interrupt," she said rather abruptly

"but any chance of getting two cups of tea?"

Before the woman was able to respond, Liz stepped forward.

"Sarah, love, this is Christopher, your erm, brother."

"Oh, hi, pleased to meet you," said Sarah holding out her hand. Christopher turned towards them.

"That's a bit formal. Come here. I'm your brother. Give me a hug." Christopher embraced Sarah tightly, and he could feel her squirm, uncomfortable in his grasp.

"Well, you are my half-brother and given it's the first time I have laid eyes on you, a hug seems a little over-familiar."

Liz felt the frisson of tension between the two of them and stepped forward to ease the situation.

"I'm up for a hug. Hello son, so lovely to see you again."

"Good to see you too. Let's find a seat, shall we?"

Settling in at an empty table near the window, Liz felt an inner glow, a feeling like she had never experienced before. For the very first time, she had her two babies by her side. Maternal love enveloped her, and for a moment, she thought the emotion might overcome her.

Before their conversation could begin, the waitress appeared with a tray laden with teacups and saucers, a giant teapot and slices of Bakewell Tart. "Oh great," said Christopher leaning over to take a wedge, "my favourite."

"Well, that's one thing we have in common," said Sarah helping herself to a piece.

Liz smiled. She was aware that conversation was slow between them, awkward even, but for her part, she just wanted to sit there and drink in the feeling of being with her children. She had wanted them to be together for so long but never imagined it would be as adults sitting in a café, unsure of what to say to each other.

"So, how have you been, love, since the last time I saw you?" Liz asked Christopher.

"OK. Thanks. After all these years, it took a while to sink in that I had found my birth mother - you. I haven't heard anything from Tom, which is disappointing. I was hoping I could have met up with him by now, but it's lovely to be here with you and to meet Sarah."

"I should have told you, Tom's wife had an accident, and she is in the hospital. It happened last week, so I suspect he won't have had a chance to ring you. I think he has spent most of the week by her bedside."

"Do you know what happened?"

"She fell in the garden and hit her head. I think she might be in a coma. Tom has managed the occasional quick call. I know he was very keen to set up a meeting with you, so don't take his lack of contact as a slur. I am sure he would wish to be here."

"That's reassuring. So Sarah, where do we start? Do you work?"

"Yes, I do, but I don't know why what someone does is always the first question you get asked," said Sarah grumpily.

"It's the same whenever you meet someone new. I met my new neighbour last week when I was out mowing the lawn, and that was the first question he asked me as well. Not something like how long have you lived here? Is this a nice neighbourhood? It is always what do you do? I am sure it's just a polite way of saying how much do you earn. All they want to do is compare their income to see how they measure up."

"Whoa, easy there, it was an innocent enough question. Let's try again, shall we? How long have you lived around here?"

"Sorry, Christopher, I didn't mean to bite your head off. It's just that question always annoys me."

"So I see."

"I live in Beighton, about 30 miles from here. I've

lived there for about ten years. I have two girls, Amelia, 15and Becca, who is 13. What about you? Any family?"

"One girl, Amy, 16, but I am divorced, and she lives with her mum in London. I don't get to see her that often, which a real shame is. Now she has hit her teens, she is not that bothered about coming to see her poor old dad, and it's awkward for me to go down there."

"Yes, that must be tough. I can't imagine being apart from the girls."

"I know only too well what it is like living apart from someone you love. Wondering what they are up to, whether they are alright, missing out on all the important milestones in their life. Whatever you do, Christopher, you need to try and see your daughter as often as you can. You will never forgive yourself if you lose touch with her," said Liz.

"I know you are right, mum – is it alright that I call you mum?"

Of course, it is, son. I've waited fifty years to hear you call me that."

"I know you are right, mum, but it is difficult. I won't give up on her, though. So tell me more about you, Sarah? What sort of things are you into?"

" I don't have a great deal of time for hobbies, what with working and ferrying the girls around to all their after-school clubs and sports, but I do enjoy baking, and I read whenever I can. I like a good crime novel, and of course, I watch TV and go to the cinema when we can. Fairly mundane family life, I suppose."

As soon as she had finished her sentence, Sarah wondered if it sounded like she was rubbing it in that she had a family life and Christopher didn't. She hadn't meant it that way. She was suddenly conscious of how difficult it was to make conversation with someone new.

"You have a good life, though. You are happy?"

"I guess so. You don't always recognise happiness at the time, do you? It tends to be that you notice it more when you are not. "

"Sarah, come on," interjected Liz, "you have a beautiful big house, two cars, and two lovely children. You go on a foreign holiday at least once a year. I think you can safely say you have a good life."

"There's more to life than just material things, mum."

"I know that, but I never thought you did," Liz laughed.

For the next hour, conversation flowed more freely. Mother, son and daughter shared anecdotes from their lives, and gradually, barriers began to come down. Before leaving, Sarah extended an invitation to Christopher to come for Sunday dinner sometime soon so that he could meet her husband and children, something she had not envisaged doing when she had first set off to the café.

Sarah was surprised to admit that she liked her half-brother. He was someone she wanted to get to know better. He seemed warm and witty. She empathised with his family situation and could see the pain in his eyes when he mentioned his daughter. Sarah couldn't bear the thought of not having daily, if not hourly, contact with her two; she was positively dreading the day when they would leave her to go to university or wherever their path would take them.

Did this mean she had been too hard on her mother when she had first told her about Christopher, she wondered? Sarah couldn't deny her mother's news had been a shock, but there was more to it than that.

Growing up, Liz had been at pains to keep Sarah on the straight and narrow. Her mother had done everything possible, short of buying a chastity belt to ensure Sarah didn't do anything to jeopardise her chances of going to university and getting a career. As it was, Sarah did enjoy the company of men from a relatively early age but getting pregnant was a repulsive thought to her as it was to her mother, just for very different reasons. Until she had met Steve many years later, motherhood was not something that Sarah craved. Sarah could see with hindsight that her mum had been trying to stop history from repeating itself. She had been trying to protect her daughter so that she was free to make her way in the world and perhaps to stop her having to face the difficult decisions that had been thrust on her. At first, hearing her mother's revelation, Sarah had felt not only that her mum had been hypocritical in her zeal to keep Sarah away from men but also intensely disappointed that her mum had got pregnant at all.

Sarah had always idolised her mother, not that she would have let her know this. She loved hearing how Liz had gone to Germany and taught in a foreign language school. Sarah admired the tenacity Liz showed when taking her driving test in her sixties. She respected the way she had looked after her dad and kept a happy home. Hearing that her mum had been caught out, getting herself pregnant outside of marriage, was scandalous. She couldn't believe it of Liz. The news had shattered everything Sarah knew to be true about her mother. It had rocked her world. She wondered what else in her life from her childhood was built on lies. She still loved her mother, but she would never look at her in quite the same way.

Returning to his car Christopher was pleased with how the meeting had gone. His half-sister seemed a good type. Feisty, a trait he wondered if they had both got from their mother.

Looking at his phone, he noticed six missed calls. He knew he couldn't ignore them forever, but he wasn't in the mood for confrontation right now.

Chapter Twenty-One

Holding up the tiny dress in front of her, Cath felt like a child in a sweetshop. Everywhere she turned were cute pink pinafore dresses and miniature shoes that looked more suitable for a doll than a human. What was she doing in here? She had a legitimate reason to be browsing the rails in Baby care, but the experience was so surreal, part of her felt like an intruder. In her mind, she had decided she was having a girl. Of course, she would not know for sure for several weeks yet, and she had not got as far as discussing with Brian whether they wanted to know the baby's gender before it was born. She guessed Brian would like a girl, given he already had two boys, but she was only basing that on her preference.

Over the years, she had not given that much thought to children. She had not been that successful with her long-term relationships, so the topic had never presented itself for serious consideration. She did know that never in a million years did she think she would be single and pregnant by a married man. This was definitely not her finest hour.

The single bit, although not great, was not the problem. It was the choice of partner. She could see now the look of disgust on her best friend's face when she had told her about Brian. Despite all the years of sisterhood between them, Jessica couldn't hide the fact that sleeping with another woman's husband was something she could not forgive. Although trying to be supportive, Cath knew her best friend was struggling to know what to say. That just made her shame so much harder to bear.

Cath didn't want it to be this way, but she couldn't help who she fell in love with, could she? Now Brian had left his wife. She should be pleased, and she was. Cath was grateful that Brian loved her enough to commit to her but hated herself for being responsible for tearing him from his family and his boys. That is not who she wanted to be. All she could imagine was the conversation in the pub when Jessica told the others what she had done. Then there was the small matter of her parents.

At what point did she break the news that they were about to become grandparents? She knew the minute she told them that her mum would want to hop straight on a plane and come over. They wouldn't usually make another trip from Spain so soon, having been over for Christmas, but this was different. Her mum loved babies. She spent hours telling Cath about the feeding habits of random friends' and neighbours' offspring. Cath usually nodded or made polite noises down the phone as her mum spoke. She would be off the scale with excitement at the prospect of having her first grandchild. There would be the inevitable disappointment when they found out that Cath wasn't getting married and the shock of finding out she had taken another woman's husband. God, why did she have to fall for a married man!

Moving further around the shop, she started to consider whether she should start making some purchases. Now she had passed the 12-week point, and it was time to face facts. The baby would soon be here, and one way or another, she needed to be prepared. She wasn't the most organised person in the world, and whilst it went against all her instincts, she ought to sit down and plan out exactly what needed doing before the birth.

Leaving the shop, two bulging carrier bags by her side, Cath determined that it was time for Operation Baby when she got home, which probably included a phone call home.

Chapter Twenty-Two

Brenda had been in the hospital for over two weeks when Tom got a message that the consultant wanted a word. It had been the longest two weeks of Tom's life. He had sat by his wife's side as long as he could each day, holding her hand and looking into her blank face. Dementia had already taken away the woman he knew and loved, but now she was heavily sedated and unable to talk. Every time he squeezed her hand, he willed her to open her eyes and smile at him.

Tom arrived at the hospital with Brian and Julie and ushered into a side room where they were joined by Mr Holsworth, the consultant overseeing Brenda's treatment.

"I'm pleased to say that the swelling in Brenda's brain has reduced to the point where we will be able to bring her round," he said.

Tom sighed. "Thank God. I thought you were going to say something terrible."

"We are not out of the woods yet, Tom, but it is a positive step forward. Brenda will need a great deal of care over the coming weeks, and I would like to suggest that she goes to a hospice where she can receive the medical care she needs. I know you all want to get her home as soon as possible, but she will need close monitoring, and I would urge you to consider a hospice, at least in the short term."

Tom looked at his son and daughter. "What do you think, Julie?"

"I think we have to listen to what Mr Holsworth is telling us, dad. You know how hard it is looking after mum when she is well, but if she needs round the clock supervision and medication, there is no way you are going to cope alone. I think it is for the best."

"Brian?"

"I agree, dad. It seems like the sensible solution right now." "OK then, what happens now?"

"I can get the ball rolling for you and put you in touch with Beauview Hospice. It is a wonderful place, and Brenda will be in the very best hands. I know this is tough, Tom, but you are making the right decision. Feel free to stay in the room a little longer if you want to talk. I'll be in touch when I've spoken to the hospice."

Mr Holsworth left the room, taking with him all Tom's hopes of a positive outcome. He knew from a practical point of view that Brenda going to the hospice was probably the most sensible option, but he couldn't help feeling that this was the end. After all, a hospice was somewhere people went to die. He couldn't believe his beloved Brenda was on the brink of death. A few weeks ago, she laughed and joked with the grandchildren and here she was, now fighting for her life. It was so unfair. Of all the people in the world, why was it always the nice ones that suffered? Murderers and rapists never seemed to die of cancer or get dementia. It was always the loving mothers and the hardworking fathers, people who had scrimped and saved their whole lives to put food on the table for their families. Tom's stomach lurched. He felt sick. Turning to look at his son and daughter, he was suddenly very aware of what Brenda's death would mean for them. They were close to their mother. Both would have to contend with the loss of a parent and the loss of a grandma. It was too much to bear. Tom began to sob uncontrollably.

"Oh, dad, it's OK," said Julie putting an arm around her father.

"It doesn't have to be for long. I'm sure mum will be home again before long."

"I know you mean well, love, but I think we all know that once Brenda goes into that hospice, there will be no coming out."

"That's a bit drastic, dad," chimed Brian.

"Just being realistic, son. I think we all have to face facts. It is going to be a hard time for all of us. No point pretending. It's the next chapter, and sadly, for your mum, it could be the last."

"Come on, dad. We'd better start heading home. We have got a lot to sort out, and I need to be thinking about collecting Zane from school."

"Let's go to the canteen first, can we? I could do with a decent cup of coffee and a sandwich."

As Tom opened the door onto the corridor, he saw Mr Holsworth in conversation with another man.

"Mr Beresford, this gentleman was just looking for you."

174

"Oh?" Said Tom perplexed, "I'm sorry, do I know you?"

"No. I'm Christopher, I'm your..."

"Christopher? What on earth are you doing here? It's a hospital, for God's sake, not a cafe. My wife is lying on the other side of those doors in a coma. What on earth possessed you to come here?" Tom's voice was getting louder and more anxious.

"I didn't mean to upset you, Tom. I just thought if you were having a hard time, I would .."

"What?" Tom interrupted. "You thought? I don't think you thought at all. How dare you intrude on such a personal situation. What did you think? That I would forget about Brenda lying through there fighting for her life and drop everything and come and play happy families with you? How did you think this was going to play out? That you could waltz in here, and I would just turn by back on my family and throw myself into your arms. My long lost son?"

"I think you ought to go, mate?" Said Brian moving forward towards Christopher.

"Don't mate me."

"Look, we are all tired and emotional. Christopher, I'm Julie, and this is Brian. You'll have to forgive us, but we have only known of your existence for 48 hours, and the last thing we expected was to meet you and certainly not in these circumstances. Why don't you join us for a coffee? We were just on our way to the canteen."

"You two go if you want," said Tom. "Brian,

drive me, home son. I can't cope with this right now."

Brian looked at Julie, who smiled and nodded. "I'll see you later, dad, OK?"

Brian ushered his father away. Watching the two walk down the corridor, Julie was struck by how old her father suddenly looked. The strain of the last few days was taking its toll, and having the prodigal son turn up at the hospital was too much. She turned to Christopher.

"I can't believe you thought coming here was a good idea."

"Maybe it wasn't one of my better moves, but when Liz told me about Tom being at the hospital, I just wanted to offer him some comfort."

"Don't you think that is what we were doing? Did you think you could pitch up here out of the blue and what, walk in and put your arms round your long lost dad, and everything would be OK?"

"Alright, I get it. I was naive. I'm sorry. I shouldn't have come. Do you want me to go?"

"No. We might as well have that coffee. Come on. The canteen is down this way."

Pushing open the doors to the canteen, Christopher couldn't help but think how much he hated hospitals. He used to think it was the smell, but there was no one dominant odour right now. It was, he concluded, the starkness of the place. The harsh lighting in the canteen was casting huge shadows onto the bland Formica tables. People were talking in hushed tones, hugging polystyrene cups of murky brown liquid. Unappetising sandwiches pressed up against huge beige slabs of cake in the glass counter, each piece tightly wrapped in cling film.

"Two coffees, please."

"Cups or mugs?"

"Cups, please."

"Cheers," said Julie taking a cup and raising it in Christopher's direction. "Here's to new beginnings."

"What makes you say that?"

"Well, my dad always says your life is like a book. My mum will be moving to a hospice, and dad says that's her next chapter. It will be a new beginning for all of us. Mum in the hospice, dad living on his own and for you, meeting your new family. It's a new beginning for all of us."

"So, you still think I have a future as part of the family then? I haven't blown it completely?"

"It might take dad a little while to come round. He's focused more on mum right now, but I know how much it means to him to have fathered a child. I can't see him missing out on getting to know you."

"What about you? It must be a bit weird for you too?"

"Yes. I can't deny it was certainly a shock when we found out about you. Brian and I are adopted, not that that has ever been an issue, but knowing all of a sudden that dad had a biological child did make me feel a bit uneasy."

"Uneasy? Why do you say that?"

"I don't know. Maybe that isn't the right word, but I suppose I did have a moment of wondering whether dad would want to know us now he has a biological child."

"I can't imagine he would turn his back on you, but then again, I am not in a position to comment, am I? I don't know anything about him as yet, only the snippets that Liz has told me."

"That's weird as well. We have only just found out about Liz. Fancy meeting up after all those years. You couldn't make it up. What's she like, Liz?"

"Nice. It was odd going to meet my mother for the first time at my age. I didn't know what I felt about her. I was kind of hurt at the thought of being given away, but then, having had a kid of my own, I could imagine how hard that must have been for her. I believe her when she says she has never stopped thinking about me. My kid lives with her mum in London, and I can't stop thinking about her. I know I can see her whenever I want. Not ever seeing your kid again must be truly heartbreaking. She has certainly made me feel welcome, and I have met her daughter too, Sarah. She seems to be taking things in her stride. She's invited me over for Sunday dinner."

"Oh, so that's good. At least it's going well on one side of your family." Julie smiled.

"So, you got any kids?"

"Yes, a son, Zane. He's five and is a complete

live wire. He runs me ragged. How old is your son? Daughter?"

"Daughter, Amy. She's 16 going on 30. She's got a typical teenager's mouth on her at the moment. First, we divorced and then last year, her mum remarried, and I think it has hit her harder than she is letting on. It's all teenage bravado at the moment.

"Where's Zane now? At home with his dad?"

"Er, less of the Spanish inquisition if you don't mind."

"Sorry. I didn't mean to pry. I was just wondering if you want to go and get a beer somewhere as this coffee isn't hitting the spot."

"I suppose we could adjourn around the corner to the Black Bull. It's not every day you meet your long lost half-brother."

*

"Two pints, please, mate. Thanks."

"Thanks, Christopher, cheers."

"Cheers, here's to happy families."

"Well, families anyway, not sure they are always happy ones," corrected Julie.

"You not happy? Sorry, am I prying again?"

"It's OK. It's tough at the moment with all that is happening to mum. The last year has been challenging as dementia has taken hold. She has gone downhill quickly, and it is sad to see. Dad's been a trooper. He has had to step up and has done a brilliant job of caring for her. Then the fall was such a shock. We thought she had just bumped her head, but it turned out to be much more severe. She has had a bleed on her brain, and it doesn't look like she will make a full recovery. They want her to go into a hospice. I think it is the right thing, but dad's struggling with the idea. He is going to hate living on his own.

"Then there is my own life. I am a single mum, which for the most part, I don't mind, but Zane's dad has come back on the scene, and well, there is a little bit of me that thinks getting back together with him and settling down might not be the worst idea I ever had. Oh God, listen to me prattling on. Sorry, I don't know where all that came from. I don't normally spill my guts to a stranger."

"I'm glad you did. It's nice to know someone else's life is as messy as mine," quipped Christopher. "Shall I get us a couple more?"

"Yes, why not."

Chapter Twenty-Three

After dropping off Zane for a play date with his friend Aaron, Julie drove the forty miles to where she had agreed to meet Christopher. It was Saturday morning, and she had a hundred and one other things she should be doing, but the thought of stealing a couple of hours for herself to have a coffee with her new big brother was too much of a temptation to ignore. The washing could wait.

Christopher took the mug of steaming coffee and made his way to the squishy sofas in the corner of the cafe where he could see Julie was sitting, flicking through a magazine. As he approached, she looked up and smiled.

"Hey."

"Hey."

Christopher leaned over and planted a soft kiss on Julie's cheek.

"How are things? Any change at home?"

"Nothing much has changed for dad. We are just waiting for a date to move mum to the hospice. He is dreading it, but I think he is also getting used to the idea that it is in her best interests. I know he is going to miss her like mad."

"He'll be able to visit when he wants, won't he?"

"Of course, but when you have lived together as man and wife for God knows how many years, it is a heck of a change to have to go and visit someone in a different town."

"Yes, poor Tom, it must take some getting used to. I still wish I could lend him my support. Do you see any chance of me seeing him any time soon?"

"Not really, Christopher. Under any other circumstances, I am sure he would not have hesitated to see you. When he told us about you, he was planning a meeting. You will just have to be patient, I'm afraid. Once he has got mum settled in the hospice, I am sure he will be in touch. And anyway, in the meantime, you have me and Brian to get to know."

"Yes, although I'm not sure about Brian. I don't think he likes me."

"Don't be daft. You have to remember how much of a shock all this is to us. After all these years, finding out dad has a biological child is a big deal, especially as we were adopted. Brian will come round. Besides, he has a lot going on at the moment. He has just found out that the woman he has been having an affair with is pregnant. He's left his wife and two small boys to go and support her, but I am not sure he believes that is what he wants. His poor wife has taken it badly, and of course, the boys miss him like mad."

"When you put it like that, I guess I am not the top of his priorities. I know only too well what it is like being separated from your children, well, child, in my case. I'd give anything to have Amy back in my life. That must have taken some doing to walk away from his boys. At least I have got the other side of the family. I've met Liz again and her daughter Sarah who was very nice. I guess I need to be grateful for how things have panned out so far. It is more than I ever thought I would find."

"Bet you didn't bargain for all our baggage when you made contact with Liz?"

"I suppose I didn't stop to think about it that much. After a lifetime of wondering who my parents were and why I had been adopted, I couldn't wait to meet Liz. I didn't give that much thought to the wider family. Pretty selfish, I suppose. What about you? Have you ever wondered about your real parents?"

"Of course, I've wondered about them all my life. As a child, it bothered me greatly to think that someone could give me up. I wondered what on earth I had done that was so bad that they didn't want me. I was pretty shy as a girl, and I think it was down to a fear of rejection. Even now, I'm not great at relationships. I tend to dump men before they can dump me." Julie paused. She had surprised herself with the level of honesty with which she was engaging Christopher. Julie wasn't sure what it was, whether it was their shared experience of both being orphans or whether he was just a good listener. Still, she wasn't usually as quick to divulge her innermost feelings to a relative stranger. He didn't seem fazed by her honesty. As he stretched out his legs in the chair opposite, he seemed relaxed and ready to listen some more.

"Is that what happened with Zane's dad? You

dumped him?"

"You don't sugar coat things, do you?" The directness of the question caught Julie off guard.

"Sorry. I didn't mean to pry. I was just picking up on what you said."

"It's OK. Guess you have hit a bit of a nerve with that one. Zane's dad was probably the exception to the rule. He was the one that got away. I hadn't planned to get pregnant, but I knew I wanted to keep the baby once it happened. I loved Marcus and hoped he would be equally happy with the news, but sadly, I was wrong. He was doing well in his career, and the last thing he wanted was to be tied down. He left me, us, to follow his corporate dream. I was distraught."

"Didn't you say he was back on the scene?"

"He sent me a note to say he was back in town, but I haven't replied."

"So you kept in touch?"

"Not much. He pays maintenance for Zane, and he writes from time to time to let me know where he is for emergencies, but after he left, I haven't spoken to him."

"It can't have been easy for you to bring up Zane alone."

"No, it has been tough. Mum has been a great help and dad since he retired. They have always been very supportive and ready to help with babysitting. I wouldn't have been able to go back to work if it hadn't been for them."

There was something deeply comforting in the

way he listened to her. She had never felt quite so at ease with anyone, particularly a man. Usually, men only paid her this much attention when they were trying to get her into bed. This was definitely a new experience.

"Can I meet him?"

"Zane?"

Julie was taken aback by the question. She usually did everything possible to shield Zane from her men friends, but this was different. Christopher was family, but still, it was early days, and she didn't know him.

Although, for some reason, she did think she could trust him.

"I don't see why not," she finally answered. "Let's leave it a few weeks and see how things pan out with dad, but I am sure we can work something out."

"Do you fancy another cuppa?"

"Christopher, I had better be getting back home. I've got a load of jobs to do, and I need to look up a plumber as I've got a bit of a leaky shower that I need to get fixed before it makes a mess of the ceiling below."

"Why don't I take a look for you? I'm quite handy like that, and there's not much I can't do around the house."

"It's a long way. Don't you have anything else you need to be doing?"

"No. I've got a card session with some mates tonight, but I've no plans for the rest of the afternoon. Are you parked outside? I can follow you back to yours if you want?"

*

"I can have that fixed in no time for you," Christopher said as he came down the stairs and rejoined Julie in the living room. "I just need to nip to the shop for some sealant, and then it's a five-minute job."

"If you are sure you don't mind." Julie wasn't used to this kind of service, and it had been a long time since any man in her life had been so helpful. She usually was the one doing all the running around.

"Not at all. I noticed a huge DIY place on the ring road when we drove in. I'll be back in no time. You might as well get it fixed. As you said, you don't want to end up with a big stain on the ceiling or worse."

"OK. Thanks. I'll make us some sandwiches for when you get back."

"Great. See you in a few minutes."

As she watched Christopher drive away in his shiny, big BMW, she couldn't help wondering what had gone wrong between Christopher and his wife. He seemed an ideal catch from what little she had seen so far. Was there a darker side to him that she had not yet seen, or was it his wife who had proved too difficult to live with? Having had no success herself with relationships, Julie was endlessly fascinated by other people.

She had watched with admiration how Brenda had coped over the years: left alone for months at a time to raise her and Brian whilst their dad was at sea. She remembered the tension in the air when Tom returned home. As children, they had been so excited to greet their father, but it always seemed to take Brenda a few days to get used to having another adult in the house. She would go through the motions of making a big fuss, but their conversation would be polite rather than intimate. They would dance around each other, neither wanting to say or do something to upset the other. After a few days, the atmosphere would clear, and laughter would return. Then all too soon, it was time for Tom to pack his bags again and head back to port, and so it had continued.

Brian was no role model, going off having an affair when he had a beautiful wife and two gorgeous sons at home, and even saintly Cheryl had done the dirty. That had been a shock.

Cheryl was the epitome of the devoted wife and mother. She was the very last person she would ever have thought capable of cheating. Her friends were no better. Single, divorced, separated and abandoned, not one of them could claim to know the secret of maintaining a long and healthy relationship. Were they all doing something radically wrong, or were real life and long-term monogamous relationships only found in fiction? Quite a depressing thought, she concluded.

A few minutes later, Christopher returned with the sealant and a bunch of flowers and a large bag of sweets.

"I thought you might like these to cheer you up," he said, presenting Julie with the flowers. "I just won £25 on a scratchcard, so I thought I would treat you, and these are for Zane."

He then set about repairing the shower. He was right; it didn't take him long. He then joined Julie on the sofa and tucked into the cheese and pickle sandwiches she had rustled up and which she had laid out on a plate on the pale wooden coffee table in front of them. She had never bothered with a dining table. The house was small, and there never seemed any point in being that formal for just her and Zane. The two of them were pretty happy eating meals balanced on their knees or sitting on the floor.

If he thought it odd, Christopher didn't comment. He seemed at home huddled next to Julie on the modest two-seater sofa. It had always seemed spacious enough for her and the tiny frame of a toddler, but now, with the manly bulk of someone over six feet pressed up against her, it suddenly felt woefully inadequate.

She needn't have worried, though. Half an hour later, they had settled in quite nicely. Julie had put a film on, and they had managed to rearrange their bodies so that they both lay comfortably, slightly entwined on the faithful grey corduroy couch. When the film finished, and he turned his head to kiss her, it seemed the most natural thing in the world.

*

Later that night, when Christopher met up with his card buddies, he was feeling lucky. He was still buzzing from the time he had spent with Julie, and his win on the lucky dip had to be a good omen. The six men had been meeting up to play poker every Friday night for as long as Christopher could remember, probably going on six years at least. It had to be at least that long because it was one of a long list of things of which his ex-wife had disapproved. It was harmless enough. They had a few beers, smoked - depending on whose home they were in - and played cards until they were either too drunk to continue or had nothing left to bet. Sadly, Christopher's good fortune didn't prevail, and by the time the men finally called it a night, he was drunk and considerably deeper in the red.

Chapter Twenty-Four

It had been almost a month since Tom had last seen Liz. He was worried that she would think he had given up on her and Christopher. He still couldn't get over him turning up like that at the hospital. Had he been too hard on him? He hoped he hadn't blown it with him, but at the same time, he still hadn't quite forgiven him. What was he thinking, barging in on such a private family moment? Under what circumstances was that the appropriate time to introduce yourself to your long lost father?

Then again, what if it had been the other way round? What if Tom had found out that Christopher was at the hospital watching over his sick child? Would Tom have gone running over there to help? He couldn't answer that one. He was older than Christopher and had experienced a bit more of life, but he couldn't honestly say how he would have reacted. He did want to put it behind them and start again. It was just that he didn't have the headroom to think about much else until he could get Brenda settled into the hospice.

He loved Brenda so much. It was true that he had taken her for granted. He had always assumed she would be there waiting for him when he came back from the long stints at sea; Tom never stopped to consider what she had had to contend with bringing up two children alone whilst he was away. She had done an excellent job raising the kids, and the home was always spotless. Once he had retired, they had so many plans to travel together - he had promised to take her to some of his favourite haunts so that she could see for herself the places he had described when he came home. They had started to enjoy days out together and with the grandchildren. They had so much to look forward to - and then she got ill. Now all their plans were fantasies. He was on the brink of losing her, and it hurt. It was hard to contemplate a future without her.

He wondered whether he should drop Liz a note to let her know that he was thinking about her and that he did plan to see her again as soon as he could. Yes, that was it. He walked over to the corner of the living room. He had fashioned office space by moving a bookcase and replacing it with a bit of a desk and chair. There was just room for a few box files above the desk and some bits of stationery. The kids never had anything like it when they were young. They used to have to do their homework sprawled on their beds or at the dining room table. He grabbed a pad of Basildon Bond and thought about what to say.

Dear Liz,
So sorry I have not been in touch for a while. I am still waiting for Brenda's date to go to the hospice, hopefully, any day now. I hope things are OK with you? Have you patched things up with Sarah? I hope we will be able to see each other

again soon.

Tom

He thought for a minute or two whether he should
have put 'love Tom' and whether he should have
added a kiss on the bottom, but he decided it was
probably better for now that he kept it simple. He
sealed the envelope and sat back. It was strange,
he thought, but he had loved these two strong,
elegant, determined women with equal passion all
his adult life.

It was true Liz had been his first true love, and he
was devastated when she left him at the tender age
of 18. He had continued to mourn losing Liz until
the minute he had clapped eyes on Brenda. Even
then, his feelings for Liz didn't disappear, they just
moved to the back of his mind whilst this
wonderful, new apparition took centre stage.

Brenda was six years his junior. She was on a
work's outing in Portsmouth with some girls from
the office when he had first plucked up the courage
to go over and start talking to her. It was such a
common occurrence for young women to be
chatted up by hordes of sailors that Brenda had not
been impressed by his smart uniform or well-
presented appearance. Brenda might have been
playing it cool, but Tom was smitten. She was
slightly plumper than most of the other girls, but
that hadn't bothered him in the slightest. Her eyes
were mesmerising, deep brown, piercing yet
inviting. She also had the most charming smile and

a laugh which made his heart flutter every time he managed to crack that protective shield she had got used to placing around her. They had taken it easy.

In contrast to the majority of her friends, theirs was a slow romance. Interrupted at regular intervals by Tom's training and then first posting overseas, it was getting on for two years before they could finally tie the knot. Then they had moved north.

Brenda had continued to shine brightly at the centre of his universe ever since. Would it be the case that Liz would once more become the dominant light in his life as Brenda moved into the hospice? It was too soon to say, but Tom knew it was a distinct possibility.

Under very different circumstances, he would have had no hesitation about trying to woo Liz. He couldn't believe how natural it had felt to talk to her after almost half a century apart. He felt completely at ease in her company. It was true that they had both changed and experienced very different things throughout their lives, but meeting up again was somehow like coming home. He could quite easily have pulled her close and given her a loving embrace, but instead, he had made do with a peck on the cheek.

He grabbed his coat and took the short walk to the postbox.

Chapter Twenty-Five

Tom replaced the receiver on the telephone. A week tomorrow. That was the date they had said for moving Brenda into the hospice. He couldn't decide how he felt. He knew it was the right thing for Brenda to ensure she got 24-hour care, but it was so sad that she was leaving the family home. Tom knew that the house would never feel like a home again. It didn't seem two minutes since he and Brenda had come to look around the house. They were newly married, and they were so excited at the prospect of buying their own place. They had fallen in love with the house as soon as they had seen it. It was large and spacious, and they could imagine filling the rooms with children and happiness. Brenda had been the perfect wife.

She had bought material and made curtains and cushions, transforming the empty shell into a cosy home. Every time they went on holiday or a day out, she would return with a souvenir that would take pride of place on the mantelpiece or one of the many shelves. Soon she filled every square inch of the house with memorabilia. Tom didn't mind. His wife was happy; the children had an excellent home to grow up in, and that was all that mattered to him. Spending so much time away from them all at sea, he was always surprised and delighted when he walked back through the front door and saw the jumble of children's toys, paintings and assorted bric-a-brac.

Now there would just be him, alone in the house with all those memories.

He needed to tell the children the news. "Jules, it's dad. How are you doing?"

"Hi Dad, I'm OK, thanks, you?"

"Yeah, I'm OK. The hospice has just confirmed a date for when your mum can move in. A week tomorrow. Do you think you would be able to get the day off work to help?"

"Of course, dad. Don't worry. I am sure Brian and I can both be there to help you. Have you told Brian yet, or do you want me to?

"No, if you could let him know, that would be great. Julie, how did you get on with Christopher? I was just wondering if he had left a contact number with you when you left him at the hospital?"

Julie could feel her heart beating inside her chest. Did she just blush at the mention of his name? It was a good job that they were talking on the phone and not in person. Otherwise, her dad would have read something in her reaction. Should she feel this guilty? Had she done anything wrong? OK, so they had kissed, but they were not blood relatives, so that was acceptable, was it? She had a hundred and one things racing through her head.

"Yes, he did leave his number and his address, and he wanted to make sure you got them." She was trying her best to sound nonchalant.

"I just wanted to get in touch with him and

apologise for giving him such a hard time at the hospital. Hold out a bit of an olive branch."

Julie was impressed. She had no idea that her dad would have had such a change of heart so quickly. She didn't feel that she could tell him that she had seen Christopher once or twice since the hospital and that they were getting on rather well. Better to let him form his own opinion, she thought. She knew Christopher would be thrilled by the development.

"I'll dig it out and ring you back. You will have to let me know how you get on. Are you planning to meet Christopher?"

"I'll give him a ring and suss him out."

Julie was amazed but at the same time a little apprehensive about the prospect of the two of them meeting up. She hoped to God that Christopher would be discreet. She would love to be a fly on the wall at that meeting, she thought.

*

Later that day, when Tom finally plucked up the courage to phone Christopher, he didn't get the reaction he was expecting. Far from being pleased to hear from Tom, Christopher was openly hostile. He raged at Tom for the way he had shunned him at the hospital. When he was finally able to end the phone call, Tom slumped to the floor. The rejection felt like a hot poker plunging into his heart. The last thing he wanted was to alienate his

196

son or give him the impression that he was a nuisance. God the years Tom had dreamed of having a child of his own. He would never forgive himself if he had hurt Christopher. Tom was desperate to reach out to his son and tell him how much he was loved, even though they were strangers. Now Tom wondered if he would ever be able to make things right again.

Tom walked into the bedroom and sat on the bed. Brenda's nightie was lying on the pillow just as it always had for the last umpteen years. He picked it up and clutched it tightly to his chest. She would never set foot in this bedroom again. He would never watch her change into the nightie, sit at the dressing table and apply her face cream, or feel the warmth of her body against his as she slid between the sheets next to him. She had not even had a chance to say her goodbyes. She had left the family home in an ambulance when she had banged her head in the garden, not knowing that she would never again see the rooms where the children had grown up or the kitchen that had been the focal point of so many family dramas. She never got to say goodbye to the garden that she had so lovingly tended over the years or to the pets buried under the apple tree in the far corner. She didn't get to say goodbye to the neighbours or him. Now becoming accustomed to the sensation, Tom felt the yearning pit in his stomach and the warmth of the tears streaming down his face. His precious Brenda was never coming home.

Chapter Twenty-Six

Removing a piece of paper from the envelope that someone had shoved under his front door, Christopher looked at the stark warning.

The message couldn't spell out his predicament any more clearly. 'Sixty grand by Friday or else.'

At first, he thought he was still asleep, but gradually, he realised that this nightmare was genuine.

Beads of sweat gathered at his temples. His heart raced. He knew he had pushed his luck to the limit. It was the 'or else' that worried him. He knew what Jake Sylvester and his henchmen were capable of. It wasn't his safety that bothered him but the thought that they might track down his family. He would never forgive himself if anything happened to Amy. How had he let things get this bad? Right now, he would be lucky to scrape together sixty pounds, let alone sixty thousand.

Last night had got messy. He had been winning for the most part. If only he had managed to win that final hand. It wouldn't have cleared his debt, but at least he could have offered Jake something as a bargaining chip. He had tried to blot out his disappointment with beer. He couldn't remember the others leaving, but the carnage that greeted him in the living room this morning suggested it had been a heavy night.

He took a swig of whisky then instantly regretted it. His head was still pounding from last night, and the last thing his body needed was more alcohol. He was running out of options. He could try and win the money back before Friday, but that didn't seem very realistic the way his luck was going. He had nobody who could lend him that sort of money, and he had asked once too often. His only option was to see what he could sell, starting with his car. Even willing to sacrifice his precious BMW, Christopher knew he was expecting a miracle to be able to raise the money by Friday. He would have to hit the casino tonight and hope for the best.

He wondered whether there was any way he could borrow the money from his 'new family.' It would get him out of a sticky situation, but how could he drop into conversation that he needed sixty thousand pounds? He had only just met them. The last thing he wanted right now was to chase them away. His wife and daughter had left him, and he didn't want to risk alienating anyone else.

It was then that the phone rang. Unless the person on the other end was ringing to tell him he had just come into sixty grand, he didn't want to know.

*

The minute Christopher put the phone down, he instantly regretted what he had just said and how he had behaved. He was kicking himself for being so stupid and childish. Tom had rung to make amends, and Christopher had thrown it back in his face. Instead of taking the opportunity to get to meet Tom finally, he had derided him for the way he had treated Christopher when he had turned up at the hospital. Not only that, but for some inexplicable reason, Christopher had spouted absolute venom. He had blown it now. So much for borrowing money, he would be lucky if Tom ever wanted to speak to him again. God, he could be so stupid. Christopher reached for the bottle of whisky and took another large swig.

*

Christopher had been in the casino for a couple of hours. He felt at home there, in the subdued lighting. He liked how the baize of the tables cast a subtle emerald hue over the surroundings. The smartly dressed croupiers made him feel like he was mingling with people who had made it in the world.

He had scraped together enough cash to buy himself a place at the table, but he needed a drastic turnaround in his fortune if he was going to walk away with a decent payout. He could feel the eyes of the bouncers watching his every move as they circled the tables. He also knew other eyes were also monitoring him via the CCTV. He was a bit too well-known here. Perhaps he should have chosen somewhere new where they didn't know his track record but coming here was comforting. It was where he had won and lost his life savings many times over. When things went his way, he was the toast of the room, and when they didn't, the staff would dust him down and console him with words of encouragement or a gentle reminder to watch his step.

Only this time, his luck had finally run out. He had to face the consequences. There was no way he could pay his debt to Jake Sylvester, and another couple of days would not make any difference. That night, in the alley at the back of the casino, Jake's boys delivered a message in the only way they knew. It didn't wipe out what he owed. It was simply Jake's way of showing Christopher he meant business. Christopher could only imagine what Friday would bring.

Battered and bruised, Christopher crawled to the end of the alley, where he managed to flag down a taxi that took him to the nearest hospital. The following day he called one of his card-playing buddies to collect him and take him home.

"Whoa, Christopher, what the hell happened to you?" Asked Rick as he caught sight of his pal coming down the hospital corridor. Christopher was on crutches and was clearly in pain with every step he took.

"I had a bit too much to drink and crashed the car. Let's get out of here. Thanks for coming for me."

Christopher didn't want Rick knowing his business. He was a good enough mate to come and collect him, and he was good for a few rounds of cards once a week, but he wasn't the most reliable of mates. There was no way Christopher would let on about his debt to Jake Sylvester or the truth behind his 'accident.' Right now, he just wanted to get home and hide.

Chapter Twenty-Seven

Cautiously Christopher edged himself off the sofa to answer the knock at the door. He was confident of it not being the return of the thugs as they would not have been so subtle in their attempts to gain entry. He was, however, surprised to find Julie on his doorstep. As she took in the sight before her, Julie physically recoiled. Christopher's swollen and bruised face made him almost unrecognisable.

"My God, Christopher, what on earth has happened to you? Shouldn't you be in the hospital?" She followed him inside and took his arm to guide him back to the sofa. She could see the pain shoot through him as he manoeuvred.

What should he say? Could he risk telling her the truth, or would it send her running for the hills? If he lied, though, it could make everything ten times worse.

"It looks worse than it is. A couple of broken ribs and plenty of bruising." His eyes were fixed on the floor.

"So what happened?" She could sense Christopher was reluctant to say. "It's OK, whatever it is, we're family." She added, trying to reassure him.

"Gambling debt."

Julie wasn't sure what he would say, but that certainly hadn't entered her head. She would have guessed that he had been mugged or perhaps been the victim of a road rage incident. This was something entirely different and a first for her family. She was at a loss of what to say next. Fortunately, Christopher filled the void.

"I've let things get a bit out of hand. I owe a guy some money, and I thought I could win it back, but my luck ran out. He could see I couldn't pay him back, and this was a taste of things to come."

"You still owe him the money? Even though he's beaten the living daylights out of you? Where are you supposed to get it from?"

"That's my problem. Jake doesn't care as long as I hand it over by Friday. I dread to think what will happen then. I am just praying he doesn't know where my daughter lives."

"He wouldn't go after a child, would he?"

"His type won't stop at anything to get their money. I'm sorry, Julie. I bet you never bargained for anything like this when you came to see me. Why did you come, by the way?"

"My dad told me about the phone call he had with you. It seemed so unlike you to be nasty to him over the phone. I have tried phoning you on your mobile phone, but when I didn't get any response, I thought I would come and see if you were alright. You are not."

"I'm afraid Tom rang just at the wrong moment. I didn't mean to shout at him. I was just preoccupied."

"He will probably be able to help."

"Who? Tom? How? Why would he want to help

me? He hasn't properly met me yet, and the two occasions on which we have had any contact have ended in a shouting match."

"You don't know him. He is your father at the end of the day, and he is a lovely man. He will do anything for his family. You need to give him a chance. Why don't you throw a few things into a bag, and I'll take you back to mine. I can look after you, and we can get dad over for a chat."

"You'd do that for me?"

"Of course, as I said. We're family."

As Christopher collected up some toiletries and basics for his unexpected trip, he couldn't believe his luck. Not only was his sister offering to look after him, but she had also suggested that Tom would still be willing to help him out. If this was true, maybe he might see Saturday after all.

Chapter Twenty-Eight

"Good morning Frazier and McMahon. How can I direct your call?"

"You can direct me anywhere you want", came the unexpected and rather inappropriate reply. Cheryl did her best to keep a straight face and her professional demeanour, although she knew straight away that it was Mike on the phone, probably phoning from his mobile to make it seem like an external number. This was getting to be a habit. He had phoned several times this week, and those were just the calls she had answered. Goodness knows how many Lucy or the relief receptionist had responded to.

"I'm sorry Mr Montague isn't in this morning. Can I put you through to his secretary" she replied without missing a beat. Cheryl was keen that Lucy wouldn't pick up on what was going on. She had managed to keep their assignation quiet, but if Lucy got wind that Mike was phoning, her life would never be the same again.

"Can I see you again? I can't stop thinking about you. Say you'll meet me after work for a drink, and I promise to stop ringing."

"Yes, that's right. Mr Montague will be back tomorrow, and he is usually in the office from eight. Can I tell him who called?"

"Tomorrow, at eight? Do you want me to come round to yours again?"

"Right you are then, goodbye."

Cheryl smiled to herself. All she needed to do now was ask Brian to have the boys for the night. She was looking forward to a night with Mike and some adult conversation. Since Brian had moved out, her evenings had been filled with homework, bedtime battles with the boys and endless discussions about dinosaurs. She had always lamented how little Brian did around the home, but once she was on her own, it seemed that there was suddenly an endless call on her time. She hardly had a chance to catch her breath before it was time for bed.

Being tired didn't necessarily mean she fell asleep. Often she lay there thinking about her life and how it had come to this. What had gone wrong with her marriage? What had led Brian into the arms of Cath? Had she not been attentive enough? Was she too dull? Would Brian ever come back to them? Would she take him back? So many questions to which she still didn't know the answers. Some nights she had taken to popping a couple of sleeping tablets to help her drift off. They were the herbal kind that you could get in the supermarket, nothing sinister. They just helped to take the edge off—a couple of those and a glass of wine or two.

It was hard to know who was the most excited about spending a night at their dad's house. Archie was the first to pack his bag, and even Daniel, who rarely showed any enthusiasm for anything these days, seemed genuinely pleased to be getting out of the house for the night. As for Brian, he was over the moon when Cheryl had called to suggest the boys could go over for the night. Although the arrangement was convenient and Cheryl was looking forward to a night with Mike, she couldn't help wondering if this was what it would be like from now on. Were they another one of those families whose lives revolved around making arrangements to hand over the kids? The prospect produced a shudder down her spine, and she poured herself a comforting glass of Dutch courage.

The night with Mike was a triumph. For the first time in weeks, she relaxed and felt the tension drain away from her body. She loved the way he ran his hands through her hair as they talked. It had the same calming effect as when she stroked a friend's cat, and if it hadn't been so absurd, she could quite easily have purred. She enjoyed the sensation of feeling wanted, and the warmth of his body against hers made her feel safe.

When he put his strong arms around her and pulled her close, she felt like nobody could ever hurt her again. She remembered when Brian used to have the same effect.

Everything between Brian and Cheryl had been fine until Daniel came along. They were both overjoyed to be parents and doted on their gorgeous, dark-haired, dark-eyed beauty. Cheryl had insisted that Daniel's cot should be in their bedroom so that she would be sure to hear if he needed her in the night. Brian had happily gone along with the idea feeling equally cautious in the first few weeks about whether he would hear the baby's cries. As it turned out Daniel was so quiet, Brian often found himself tiptoeing round to his cot in the middle of the night to check that his son was still breathing.

Cheryl had been a textbook mother, doing everything possible to give her new baby the best start in life. If anything, she was too keen. She never wanted to let Daniel out of her sight and hated it when Brian was the one to cuddle him or take him out for a walk. When he was away from her, Cheryl panicked. What if something had happened to him? What if Brian dropped him or let him get too cold? Her heart would race, and sweat would start to form on her brow. Her chest would tighten, and it would become hard to breathe. Sometimes she felt like she would die before seeing her boy again.

Six months later, Brian was convinced that Daniel could now quite happily be left in the comfort of his newly created nursery. Not Cheryl, though. Every time the subject came up, she would plead for just one more week with him in their room and inevitably, the first year passed, and Daniel still hadn't spent a night away from Cheryl's side. As every waking and, no doubt, every sleeping moment was focused on her firstborn, Cheryl neglected to notice that she had paid no attention to Brian for the last 12 months.

Barely had things got back to normal when Cheryl fell pregnant with son number two. Brian was keen that they would not make the same mistake again and insisted that Archie would be fine in his brother's company in the nursery. This time there was no argument. Something changed in Cheryl's brain. Not only did she agree, but she was more than happy to let Brian tend to all the boy's needs. She had been determined to breastfeed Daniel, but she did not want to know when Archie came along. In fact, she could hardly bring herself to touch her newborn son. For her part, Cheryl felt nothing towards him. The flood of maternal love she had felt for Daniel had vanished. She felt cold towards this new stranger in her house. A very difficult six months followed, which finally saw Cheryl diagnosed with post-natal depression. The GP had been slow to recognise what was going on, and it was a further month or so before Cheryl finally got the help she needed to turn the corner. Eventually, thanks to her mother's intervention and extended babysitting sessions from Brenda and Tom, Cheryl came out of her pit of despair. Gradually she bonded with her beautiful boy and began to make a family with Brian and Daniel.

Looking back, she found it hard to imagine a time when she didn't love the very bones of both her boys. She also tended to forget the strain that those early years had put on her fledging marriage.

Chapter Twenty-Nine

Finally, today was the day that Tom would meet Christopher. Julie had been somewhat cryptic on the telephone, and Tom couldn't quite understand what had gone on, but Christopher was spending a few days at Julie's house for some reason. He was intrigued to find out more. He was also keen to make amends with Christopher. They hadn't got off to the best of starts, and he just hoped he hadn't blown it.

Arriving at his daughter's house, Tom felt unusually nervous, and he certainly wasn't prepared for the scene that greeted him. On seeing Christopher's swollen face and pained expression, Tom let out a gasp. What on earth had happened to his darling son?

"Someone has been in the wars," he quipped. "What happened to you?"

"Long story." Christopher suddenly felt embarrassed. He didn't want his first real encounter with his father to be a tale of woe. So much for wanting to impress him. He wondered if he could bluff his way out of the situation, but now Julie knew the truth; it wasn't going to be so easy.

Julie sensed the tension between the two men and tried to steer them onto more common ground.

"Dad, it seems like we have another petrol head in the family now. Christopher sounds like he is as mad about cars as you are."

"Is that what happened? Have you been in a car accident?" Tom asked.

Ignoring the question and desperate to change the subject, Julie ushered the men into the living room.

"Dad, why don't you tell Christopher about your project that is still sitting in the garage at home, waiting for some attention?"

That did the trick for a little while. Julie could see her dad physically start to relax as he regaled Christopher with the catalogue of vehicles he had owned and loved over the years and his plans to do up the 1964 Mini. He had bought it five years earlier as a retirement project, but as yet, it was still pretty much in bits. His initial enthusiasm had waned, and since Brenda became ill, he hadn't had time to give it much attention. Julie thought how nice it was to see him engaging in a conversation that made him happy. She hadn't seen him smile in months. Her mum's illness, the fall and the coma had put years on Tom, and although he had been so excited about discovering he had a son, he had had no chance yet to focus on the revelation.

For a brief moment, she could see both men were subsumed in their mutual passion and were enjoying not thinking of their all-consuming worries. Julie left the men alone and busied herself with housework. Zane was with a friend, so she took the chance to vacuum his bedroom and pick up the endless toys and clothes strewn across the floor. After an hour, she felt she could avoid the issue no longer. It was time for Tom and

Christopher to discuss what was going on.

She made a pot of tea and went back into the living room to join the men. Christopher was taking up the whole of the sofa, his legs propped up on cushions. Julie guessed her dad had come up with that particular position. She plopped the tea tray down and sat on the floor next to her father.

"Is it time to address the elephant in the room?" She asked, directing the question at nobody in particular.

Christopher winced. He knew he couldn't get away without telling Tom what had gone on, but he dreaded doing so. Unsure how Tom was going to react, the last thing he wanted was another row. The previous hour had passed so peacefully, and he had started to enjoy Tom's company, he couldn't bear the thought that it might all come to an abrupt end.

"I would like to know how you got into such a state, Christopher. If you felt you could tell me. It upsets me to see you this way, in pain."

"I got beaten up because I owe money to a thug. Gambling debt." Christopher was looking at the floor, and he couldn't bring himself to make eye contact with Tom.

"If I don't give them the lot by Friday, the worst is still to come."

"How much is the lot?"

"Sixty thousand pounds."

Tom was silent for a while as he took in the magnitude of the situation. He was doing his best to keep a blank expression and not reveal his actual shock at the figure.

"Do you feel you have to pay the money, or would we be better off going to the police?"

Christopher noticed how Tom used the word 'we' and immediately sensed Tom wanted to help, not judge.

"I owe the money fair and square. The guys I owe it to might not be legit, but I can't pretend I didn't know what I was getting myself into. Things just snowballed, and I almost won enough last week to pay them off and then I screwed up at the last minute."

"And if you pay them, will that be it, will they leave you alone? Can you trust them?"

"I think so. I know they are capable of being nasty if people cross them, but if you play fair, I think they do too."

"You'd better arrange to pay them then."

"But how? I don't have any money. That's why I got a taste of things to come."

"I'll help you, and Liz might be able to as well - if you feel able to tell her what you have told me, but there will be strings attached. We can't afford to hand over that sort of money without putting in place something to stop it happening again."

"What did you have in mind?"

"Well, I am thinking on my feet but a commitment to go to Gamblers Anonymous or counselling. Something that can help you to address the problem that has got you into this situation. What do you say?"

Christopher mulled over the proposition. He was amazed and delighted that Tom was so forthcoming with help, but he wasn't keen on disappointing Liz. Tom must have sensed what he was thinking.

"I know it's hard, Christopher but trust and honesty are the best foundations for any future relationship. If you can be open with us, then we will all do our best to help you. It's the secrets and lies that get in the way and spoil things."

"I guess you are right, Tom, thanks. I appreciate your help and Julie's for letting me stay here."

"About that. I don't think it is fair to expect Julie to look after you. She has to work, and she has young Zane to think about. Why don't you come back with me? I have got plenty of room, and now Brenda is in the hospice; I have time to look after you as well. It doesn't have to be for long. Just until your bruises have healed a bit, it will also allow us to discuss how we will get the money to the thugs that did this to you. What do you say?"

Christopher rather liked it at Julie's. In fact, he rather liked Julie. They had clicked straight away, and he felt comfortable around her. At the same time, he knew Tom was right. He didn't want to outstay his welcome, and he knew Julie was anxious about Zane getting too used to the idea of having a man around the house. Reluctantly he agreed.

*

"How's Brenda?" Christopher asked as the two men set off.

"Not so good. You probably know that she is in a hospice now. She hardly knows me these days. It's very sad."

"I'm sorry, by the way, for turning up at the hospital like that. It was rather crass of me."

"Let's put that behind us. I can't deny that it has been tough recently. It's been awful these last few weeks, ever since Brenda took that tumble in the garden. That was the start of the end. She has been going downhill fast ever since. We've had a lifetime together, and I hoped we had many more years left, but it doesn't look that way now."

"You are lucky, though, to have enjoyed such a solid marriage. I'm afraid I've made a bit of a pig's ear of mine."

"Brian said you were divorced, and you have a daughter?"

"Yes, Amy 17 going on 30. I've just had a few days in London with her as it was her birthday. It cost me an absolute fortune taking her and her friends out. You can't move in London without it costing you fifty quid. It was lovely to see her, though. They grow up so fast. It doesn't seem two minutes since I was buying her dolls and now it's jeans and make-up. I was worried that she wouldn't want anything more to do with me when she went to London, but we had a nice few days together. She's a bright girl. She wants to be a journalist. So tell me a bit about you."

"What do you want to know? You know about me getting Liz pregnant at 17. I was 18. She has probably told you that was the last time I saw her until just recently, and that was when we met up the other month there that was the first I knew about her being pregnant when we parted. I loved her back then, and I was gutted when she left. I joined the Navy soon afterwards to try and put her behind me. I did 30 years at sea. Since then, I have had one or two-bit jobs but nothing much. I worked in a garage for a while until they went bust.

"You know about Brian and Julie. I like jazz, beer and messing about with old cars. That's me. Nothing much to know. I'm quite a simple soul."

Conversation ebbed and flowed until Christopher finally fell asleep, leaving Tom to mull over the implications of his commitment to Christopher. It had been an automatic response to say he would help his son, and he did want to but had he over-promised? Could he raise that sort of money to pay off his debt? He had also been rather blasé with his suggestion that Liz would also be forthcoming with financial assistance. It wasn't his place to speak for her, and he had no idea of her situation and whether she could afford to help Christopher, let alone whether she shared Tom's motivation to do so. He was beginning to regret being so free with his solution. He would ring Liz as soon as he got back, and tomorrow he would speak to his financial adviser and see what he had to say.

*

Tom certainly knew how to cook. Half an hour after reaching Tom's house, Christopher enjoyed one of the best homemade curries he had ever eaten. There was perhaps a bit more to Tom than he gave himself credit for.

The house was warm and cosy. It was a spacious pre-war four bedroom detached that had been lovingly decorated. It was a bit too chintzy for his taste, with a plethora of ornaments on every surface, but he could see that Brenda had been house-proud. He could imagine the extended family sitting around in the good- size living room enjoying Christmas morning together. He couldn't help feeling a pang of jealousy. He would have loved to have grown up with siblings.

His had been a loving early childhood, but with just the three of them at home, there had never been much sense of occasion, although his mother had always done her best to make it feel special. It hadn't lasted long. When his father Peter died, his childhood came to an end overnight. He was just ten years old, but suddenly, he was expected to man up and take care of his mother. At the funeral, that was all anyone had said to him as they ruffled his hair or patted him on the arm. "You are the man of the house now, Christopher. You'll have to look after your mother." but who was there for him?

By the time he went to the comprehensive school, he was a loner, ripe for exploitation by anyone who came along, and they did.

First came the bullies who beat him up for his dinner money and then the gangs. It didn't take long before he was shoplifting because the gang had dared him he couldn't steal a four-pack of beer from the local off-licence, and it didn't take much longer before the stealing became more hardcore, including taking his first car. He shuddered as he remembered the distress he had caused his mother. He would never forget the look of disappointment on her face when she came to collect him from the police station. It was the same look of disappointment he had seen tonight when Tom had heard the news about his gambling debt. Tom had tried to look indifferent, but years of playing poker had taught Christopher how to notice even the subtlest of changes in someone's eyes.

*

Tom had been asleep for about two hours when he was disturbed by the sound of the house phone ringing. It was the hospice. Brenda had passed away.

Chapter Thirty

"Morning, son," Tom was sitting at the kitchen table as Christopher entered the room ", there is some tea in the pot, if you want it."

Christopher made his way to the table; his legs, still stiff and sore, made him shuffle rather than walk. He looked at Tom, who seemed smaller today, shrivelled. His face was etched with deep worry lines, and his eyes were dark pools of sadness. Was this down to him?

He sat down opposite his father and wanted to take a minute to experience this most unlikely scenario. His pleasure at finally being here with his birth father was short-lived as Tom revealed the contents of the late-night phone call. Suddenly Christopher was plunged back into the more familiar feeling of being in the wrong place. This was like him turning up at the hospital all over again. He was intruding on a private moment. A huge, significant moment in Tom's life, and he shouldn't be there. Christopher shuffled in his seat. "I'm so sorry, Tom. Do you want me to leave?"

"Leave? Why do you say that?"

"I don't want to be in the way. This is a time for you to be with your family. Do Brian and Julie know?"

"No. I haven't told them yet. There didn't seem any point ringing in the middle of the night. It wouldn't have done any good. They were better off getting some sleep. Do you think you could phone them for me? I know it is a lot to ask, but I don't think I could find the words. Don't worry about being in the way. Stay and keep me company, and we will sort something out."

"OK. If you are sure."

Two tough phone calls later, Christopher was sitting on the sofa awaiting the arrival of Julie and Brian. Despite Tom's insistence that he wanted him there, Christopher wished he was back home out of the way. He had never met Brenda, and being in her home at such a delicate time made him very uncomfortable. There was also the small matter of why he was in Tom's house in the first place, let alone why he looked like he had been in a nasty accident. If only there had been a chance to come up with a convincing story before the arrival of a never-ending stream of visitors.

Brian was the first to turn up. He didn't flinch when he saw Christopher. Julie had filled him in on what had gone on over the previous 48 hours, and he was expecting the worst. Right now, he was more concerned about his father than worrying about the antics of some newly-discovered stepbrother. Behind him was a shy-looking woman. She was hanging back in the doorway, and Christopher sensed she wanted to be there about as much as him. He encouraged her inside. She smiled weakly. The sight of Christopher covered in cuts and bruises wasn't very welcoming. He showed her into the lounge and then tumbled back onto the sofa.

"I'm Christopher, Tom's son."

"I'm Cath. Brian's partner. I wouldn't have come; only Brian asked me to drive him. He wasn't feeling up to it. The news about his mum came as quite a shock. He has taken it badly. Sorry, I am a bit nervous. I don't feel like I should be here, and I dread Cheryl turning up with the boys. I couldn't stand it if there were a scene."

"Don't worry. I am feeling like a cuckoo in the nest as well. We will hide in here and leave them to it."

Christopher couldn't help wondering what Brian saw in Cath. She was pretty enough in a plain sort of way, but she seemed scared of her own shadow. He couldn't imagine the two of them having a clandestine affair. They seemed a very unusual match. How had they met he wondered? Of course, he was dying to ask. He wanted to know all about their sordid secret. How did she feel about stealing someone else's husband, and what about dragging him away from those poor little boys? He thought better of it. He didn't want to cause any more upset. There had been enough tears for one day.

Things went from bad to worse when Julie arrived with Zane. There was another round of awkward introductions, and pregnant pauses as the strangers mentally assessed each other. Thankfully Cath offered to drive Tom, Brian and Julie to the hospice, leaving Zane alone with Christopher. The youngster was rather impressed with Christopher's mashed-up features, and he imagined his new uncle had been in a fistfight like the ones he had seen on his friend's computer game. Sadly he was closer to the truth than he would ever know. They passed a leisurely couple of hours watching TV, eating crisps, and with Christopher drifting in and out of sleep.

Soon everyone was back at the house, and a cacophony of voices shattered the peace. Then another knock at the door. It was Cheryl and the boys. Christopher braced himself for a catfight, but if Cheryl was bothered by Cath's presence, she didn't show it. She kept her focus firmly on Tom. She gave him a long hug and then sat at the kitchen table with him, holding his hand.

Now Cheryl was another matter entirely, thought Christopher. She was immaculate. What was Brian doing turning his back on such a beauty?

Brian was too busy comforting his boys to consider the true bizarreness of the situation. Here he was in his childhood home; his mum was dead, his wife and two children were in one room, and his mistress, pregnant with his baby, was next door. How had it come to this?

Cath was distraught. The last thing she wanted was to come face to face with Cheryl. As far as she was concerned, wives and girlfriends existed in different universes and were not meant to meet. This was definitely too close for comfort. She was suddenly very conscious of her swollen belly, her unwashed hair and the 'comfortable' clothes that she had thrown on that morning. She had only caught a glimpse of Cheryl as she had swooped past the open living room door, but what she had seen was a tall, striking woman with sharp features and a freshly- scrubbed appearance. Cath suddenly felt small and shabby in comparison. She was sure that was what everybody else was doing, comparing her to the gorgeous Cheryl and wondering what on earth had tempted Brian to stray. It was a question she asked herself often enough.

*

"How do you feel about dad helping out Christopher with his gambling debt?" Julie asked Brian as they were driving to the Registrar's Office.

"I am a bit pissed about it, to tell you the truth. He's only been on the scene five minutes, and dad's prepared to hand over thousands of pounds of our inheritance. We don't know what is going on, and I can't say I am too pleased about the situation. That money is ours and should be for the kids and us. What do you think?"

"I sort of agree, but then I can see it from dad's point of view as well. He suddenly finds his biological child, and he is in trouble, and I suppose it is only natural that he would want to help him."

"I get that, but what did you say Christopher owed sixty grand? Has dad even got that kind of money? It seems rather coincidental that he meets dad, and then he is taking his life savings off him the next day. That's a huge amount of money to hand over to a relative stranger, and how can we be sure it won't happen again? We don't know anything about Christopher. What if he has other skeletons in the cupboard? I would hate to see dad taken for a ride."

"Oh, come on, Brian. You can't believe that Christopher somehow engineered the situation? We can't know for sure that it won't happen again, but dad did stipulate that one of the conditions of Christopher getting the money is that he must get help, and I have said I would go along to Gamblers Anonymous meetings with him. It is in all our interests to get him out of this mess."

"That's a big commitment you are making, Jules. Are you sure you want to get involved?"

"Yes. He is our stepbrother at the end of the day, and if he is going to be part of our lives, I think this is the least I can do for Christopher and dad. Now that mum's gone, dad is going to need all of us to rally round."

"I can't believe mum has gone. The dementia was horrible, and I know she hasn't seemed like a mum for a while, but I will miss her, and the boys will too. How do you think Zane will cope?"

"I don't know. The poor little mite has had more than his fair share of people coming and going in his life. He seems rather taken with Christopher, so spending time with him might soften the blow of losing his grandma. I thought I would take Christopher back to ours again and give dad some space."

"Are you sure you can manage?"

"Yes. I think it will be nice for Zane and me to have some company, and I can help Christopher get back on his feet."

"Well, if you are sure. Come on then; we had better get this bit over. Once we have registered mum's death, I don't think there is much more we can do for now, other than start planning the funeral."

*

Around 10 pm that evening, Julie pulled up outside her home. She carried Zane from the car and settled him in his bed. Then weary from the day's demands, she flopped onto the sofa next to Christopher. He circled his strong muscular arms around her, and the two of them stayed enveloped in each other's embrace until morning.

When she finally opened her eyes and realized it was daylight, Julie was shocked to discover she had never made it to her bed. Whilst the warmth of another human being had been a great comfort to her, a night spent on the small couch had done nothing for her back. She extricated her limbs without waking Christopher and went into the kitchen to make a drink. She was cold and her body ached, so she decided to take a shower. She was enjoying the sensation of the hot water coursing over her body when she was suddenly aware of someone behind her. Instead of being startled, she gave in to the feeling of the muscular frame pressing up against her. For a few sublime moments, she allowed herself to submit to the feeling. As the tension slipped from her shoulders, her body tingled with pure pleasure.

Chapter Thirty-One

As Julie stood on the step waiting for Cheryl to open the door, she suddenly wondered if she should have phoned ahead. This was never a consideration as her brother had always insisted that she was welcome to pop round anytime and didn't have to make an appointment. But what if Cheryl was entertaining her manfriend, and this was an inconvenient time?

She need not have worried. Cheryl swung open the door and was delighted to see her sister-in-law.

"I've brought wine," said Julie, thrusting a bottle of Rioja at Cheryl.

"Great. Come in. Where's Zane?"

"I dropped him off at a friend's for the afternoon, and we've got two whole hours for a natter. Unless you have something else you need to be doing?

"No. The boys are in their rooms, but they can entertain themselves, so we shouldn't be disturbed."

The two women went through to the living room and flopped down on the sofa, Julie instinctively curling her feet under her legs and making herself comfortable. She loved Cheryl's home, although she used to feel it was like a show home compared to how clean and tidy her place was. Julie had come to realise that cleaning was just one of Cheryl's coping mechanisms, and the last thing she wanted was to make other people feel unwelcome.

"It has been ages, Cheryl since we have had a good chin wag. How are things? Are you still seeing Mike?"

Cheryl ran her fingers through her hair and shuffled on the sofa.

"Yes. We are getting on pretty well. I still miss Brian terribly. You can't be with someone for all those years and just stop having feelings for them, but I do like Mike, and he has been very kind."

"Do you think it is over then between you and Brian?"

"If you had asked me that six months ago, I would have said you were crazy but now, I just don't know. When Brian moved out to be with Cath, it was such a shock. He hurt me. I didn't for one minute think I would find someone else, especially so quickly, but here we are. Brian has made his decision, so I suppose I just have to adapt and make the most of it. The main thing is making sure that the boys are alright. They miss not having their dad around. Mike is great with them, but I am nervous about them getting too attached to him. I am not kidding myself that he is the love of my life and that we have a future together as a family. It is working OK for now, but I don't want to put him under any pressure. I don't want him thinking he has to step into Brian's shoes."

"I know what you mean. It is the same with Christopher and Zane, and I don't want Zane to get hurt either."

"Well, it is not the same, is it? I mean, Christopher is his uncle, and he's not likely to think of him as a father figure?" Julie took a big swig of her wine and didn't speak. Should she tell Cheryl how she felt about Christopher or was she better keeping it to herself? It was no good. The whole point of coming here was because she needed to unburden herself.

She took another gulp of wine.

"It is not that simple. Christopher has been spending quite a lot of time at mine, and we have become close."

Cheryl was not following where the conversation was heading.

"That is OK. I am sure Zane is old enough to understand that Christopher is only spending time with you whilst he is unwell and that once he goes back home, things will get back to normal for you two."

"No. I mean close as in intimate close. Not just in a patching him up and being supportive kind of way." Julie could sense this was not going well.

Now it was Cheryl's turn not to speak. She couldn't process what she had just heard and was at a loss about how to respond. Did Julie think this was normal, acceptable behaviour?

"Eeew, but he's your brother! You can't do that." Cheryl was horrified.

"Don't say that, Cheryl. You know we are not related by blood, and he is not my brother in the true sense of the word. If we had met at any other time, nobody would have batted an eyelid."

"Yes, but this isn't any other time. This is now. You know the situation. How do you think Tom will feel if he thinks his son and his daughter are having an affair? No. It is wrong, Julie. You have to stop it now. Does Brian know?"

Cheryl was now standing up and pacing the floor. If Julie thought she was going to have an ally in Cheryl, she had got things very wrong.

"No. I haven't told him, and he has enough going on with Cath and the baby."

"Oh, and I haven't. It didn't occur to you that I might have enough going on as well with the fact that my husband has left me for his pregnant mistress, and I am trying to look after two children on my own."

"I didn't mean it like that Cheryl, come on, don't get angry. I just thought I could talk to you about things."

"Usually you can, but this? This is something I don't think you should be sharing with anyone. It can't end well, Julie. You must see that. Your dad has just lost his wife, and this isn't the time to be dropping a bombshell like this on him."

"Do you want me to go?"

"I think you better before I say something I regret. I am sorry if you thought I would be fine with this, but I can't pretend. I might be able to forgive Brian for having an affair, but I think you have crossed the line if you think you can carry on with your brother."

"He's not my brother. OK. I can see this is making you uncomfortable, so I'll go. Please don't say anything to Brian."

"Don't worry. I think he needs to hear about this directly from you."

Julie got back into her car and put her head in her hands. She had not considered receiving such a reaction to her news. She knew it was difficult territory, but she couldn't help how she felt about Christopher. She hadn't planned to fall in love with him. Bloody typical, she thought. Of all the guys in all the world, I have to fall for my brother! *God, why am I so rubbish at finding the right guy to have a relationship with?*

Chapter Thirty-Two

"Is everything alright, Brian?" Cath asked, rolling over to face him. "You have been quiet since we got back yesterday. Are you upset about your mum, or is there something else bothering you?"

Brian stretched out his arm and pulled Cath towards his chest for a cuddle. This was his favourite part of the day, waking up next to her and enjoying an adult conversation. It was never the same at home. He had no sooner opened his eyes when the boys would come hurtling into the bedroom and bounce all over the bed. He missed them like crazy, but he definitely preferred this more sedate way of waking up and greeting the day. Of course, even this routine wouldn't last for long. Soon it would be the new baby disrupting his sleep and his early mornings. Was he ready for that again?

Right now, he just knew he had to make the most of these precious moments whilst he could. He nuzzled Cath's head. Her hair smelled of the lemon shampoo that she bought by the gallon from the local refill shop. A far cry from Cheryl's designer toiletries that graced the bathroom shelves at home, he thought.

"It is a bit of everything: losing mum, missing the boys and this whole business with dad bailing out Christopher. Dad's not said a word to me directly. If it hadn't been for Julie, I would be none the wiser. He's got some cheek that Christopher. He has only been in the family a matter of minutes, and now he is set to waltz off with our inheritance. It isn't fair."

"I thought you liked Christopher?"

"I thought I did as well, but that is just it, isn't it? We don't know anything about him. He could be a conman for all we know. Maybe this is what he does. Wheedles his way into families and then makes off with all their money. I just wish dad had consulted me before agreeing to help him out."

"Your dad doesn't have to answer to you, though. It isn't any of your business what he does with his money." Cath wondered if she had gone too far. Was Brian going to be receptive to such a comment, or would it lead to him storming out again?

"I know that" Brian pulled his arm away from Cath and sat more upright in the bed. "If this hadn't happened at the same time as losing mum, perhaps dad would have talked to me. I just don't want him to regret giving all his money away."

"Giving all your money away?"

"I know you disagree with me, Cath, but that money should be for all of us. Before Christopher came on the scene, Julie and I would be in line for that money. That is what mum would have wanted. She would want to know that her grandchildren were going to be taken care of. I could just about accept dad changing his will to include Christopher, but I just don't think it is fair that he gets the lot now, while dad is still alive."

"What if it was Julie who needed the money? Would you feel the same?"

Brian shuffled and went quiet again. Here we go. Here comes the silent treatment. Cath knew when to give up, and she had learned to spot the signals. When Brian was backed into a corner or felt he was losing an argument, he was the master of either changing the subject or closing down altogether. She decided not to push her luck and instead retreated to the bathroom and ran herself a bubble bath. Hopefully, if I leave him for half an hour, he will have come round, she thought as she lowered her unfamiliar body into the warm water.

Ten minutes later, there was a soft tap on the bathroom door, and Brian popped his head around.

"Peace offering," he said, proffering a cup of tea towards Cath. She smiled up at him. "When you are ready, do you fancy taking a drive to the coast? I'll buy you some lunch at that fish restaurant you like."

"Yes, that would be lovely. I'll not be long. Thanks for the tea."

As she enjoyed the last few minutes of her bath, Cath wondered how quickly things would change once the baby came along. She had to admit that she didn't know what kind of father Brian had been to the boys. Had he done his fair share of nappy changing, or had he left that to Cheryl? Would they still go out to lunch, or would money be too tight once she was on maternity leave? They hadn't even discussed whether she would go back to work. If she was honest, the whole baby thing had caught both of them off guard. She was pleased Brian wanted to stand by her. However, if she was honest, she knew in her heart that they weren't at the stage in their relationship where they were ready for such a commitment. She was a drifter. A hopeless case her mother had called her.

She just didn't seem to have the gift of introspection. She took what life threw at her at face value and never stopped to consider that there was an alternative.

She had drifted through school, neither failing nor excelling at anything, just blending into the background, making up the numbers. She had friends but only Jessica, who she classed as close. She had met Jessica in her first year at senior school. They were both more bookish than sporty, and their mutual dislike of PE had cemented their friendship. Although not inseparable, the pair had rubbed along ever since. Jessica, for her part, had a group of other female friends who she counted amongst her inner circle, but for Cath, Jessica was all she had. It was the same at college. She did the bare minimum to pass her course. She hung out with some of the others, but she never formed any meaningful relationships. There had been a couple of boyfriends along the way. With hindsight, she supposed she had been in love, but there had not been bolts of lightning or anything to suggest she had found 'the one.'

It hadn't been any different with Brian. She admitted being attracted to him more out of lust than love. She wasn't proud of taking another woman's husband. She hated the thought of causing Cheryl and the boys any heartache, but once she was with Brian and they had found out about the baby, she had just accepted that she would be with him, and they all had to deal with the consequences.

Things were good for the first few heady months but as Cath's belly had grown, so had her unease with the situation. As she slipped on her dress and sandals for her lunch date with Brian, she contemplated her next move.

The fish restaurant was thronging. As it was a nice day, they opted to sit outside on the expansive patio that looked out to sea. They were both wearing sunglasses, which made conversation all the more difficult. Cath needed to see Brian's eyes to know how he was feeling. Masked by his black shades, he seemed even more distant. The waiter fetched two large glasses of Pinot Gris and set them down on the table along with a glass of water for Cath and a basket containing slices of baguette and little foil-wrapped pats of butter. Cath suddenly felt famished and immediately started to unwrap one of the little parcels and spread its contents on a slice of crusty bread.

They enjoyed their main course in almost silence—both of them struggling to find a topic of conversation that flowed. By the time they were contemplating the dessert menu, Cath was losing patience.

"I am not sure this is working, Brian," she said, surprising herself with the bluntness of her declaration. *What was she doing? Did she think she could raise a baby on her own?*

Was it the hormones talking?

Brian removed his sunglasses and, for once, looked at her directly. He, too, was surprised by the outburst but somehow not wholly disappointed to hear it. Perhaps he knew she was right. Up until that moment, though, he had not allowed himself to think about it. It was true that he had been more caught up with thoughts of his other family recently: losing his mum, worrying about the boys, thinking about Christopher and missing Cheryl.

He had relegated Cath to the bottom of his list of concerns. He realized he had not been paying her the attention she deserved. The woman was carrying his child, and yet he had hardly discussed the imminent birth with her, let alone planned out their future life together. She was right. He was going through the motions. If he were honest, he would give anything to get back to his boys, and she was now permitting him to leave. He needed to grasp the opportunity before it was too late.

"I think you are right. I'm sorry, Cath. I hoped we could make a go of things, but I think I might have been a bit hasty leaving home. We hardly know each other and I hate myself for leaving the boys. I still want to be involved, though. I hope you will still let me be part of the baby's life?"

"Of course. We can work something out."

She would not have imagined having this conversation when she was picking out baby clothes a couple of weeks ago. Where had it all come from? Was she sure she wanted to let him go? She wasn't sure about anything, but she did know that bringing up a baby on her own must feel better than being the one that tore apart another family.

As they drove back to Cath's, Brian was already rehearsing the phone call he would have with Cheryl. Would she believe him when he told her that she was the one he loved? Would Cheryl take him back, or had he burned his bridges? Was she serious about the new man in her life, or was that just a temporary arrangement? He hoped to God that it was the latter.

Chapter Thirty-Three

As Tom pulled his car into the narrow driveway, he felt a rumble of butterflies in his stomach. It took him back to the feeling he used to get when he was waiting to see Liz at the youth club all those years ago. Tom glanced in the rearview mirror and ran a hand over his hair, then grabbed the flowers on the passenger seat and got out of the car. As he approached the door, he was awash with emotions. It was only a day since Brenda's death, yet it felt like years had passed since he had last seen Liz.

It was the first time he had been to her home. It had not seemed appropriate before, but now he had to get used to the idea of not being a married man. He was free to see who he wanted, and there was nobody else he wanted to see right now as much as Liz.

Liz looked amazing. Tom guessed she had made an extra special effort as he couldn't imagine she usually sat around her house looking quite so polished. He was honoured that she had made an effort for him. He gave her the flowers and then dissolved into tears, hugging her close. She held him until the tears subsided. It reminded her of her grief in the first few days of losing Frank. Their shared past and teenage love affair had forged an unbreakable bond that even fifty years of absence couldn't break. Others may think it strange that Tom would turn to the arms of a former lover on the death of his beloved wife, but to Tom, it was the most natural thing in the world. Gradually he regained his composure, and the two went inside.

Her home was warm and inviting, with little clutter. Tom admired her sense of style. There were photos of the grandchildren and paintings and bits that looked like things the youngsters had made at school but otherwise no ornaments or signs of sentimentality.

Liz made tea, and after a cautious first hour where the two of them had danced around each other, being extra careful not to say something out of turn, they had begun to relax. Eventually, Tom felt it was the right time to tell Liz about Christopher and the gambling debt, and he was surprised how calmly she took the news.

"That explains it," she said. "I knew when we first met that he was troubled by something, and that must have been what was bothering him. I can't imagine what he has been going through; he must have been so scared. What are we going to do?"

"I have offered to help him with the money. I can't run to sixty thousand, but I can probably give him enough to keep the thugs at bay."

"I'll help. Frank left me comfortable, and I would never forgive myself if something happened to Christopher. We have only just found him, and we can't risk losing him. We have to do all we can to keep him safe."

"I agree, Liz, but he is a grown man, and he is

also an addict by the sounds of things. We can give him the money this time, but we won't help him if he continues to gamble. We have to make sure he gets professional help. Plus, he has to want to change."

"Do you think he does want to change?"

"I would like to think so. Christopher seemed pretty scared at the thought of anyone tracking down his daughter, and I don't think he would do anything to put her in danger. He took quite a beating. I hope he has learned his lesson. Julie has offered to go to meetings with him if he signs up for something like Gamblers' Anonymous. They seem to have grown quite fond of each other. I don't think Brian is too happy with the situation."

"I don't think Sarah will be either, but she doesn't have to know the details, and that is our business.

"Shall I make us some dinner? You will stop for something to eat, won't you? It has been ages since we have been able to talk."

"Yes, I'd love to stay for dinner. I have nothing to rush back for."

"Why don't you make yourself comfy on the sofa? Put the TV on if you want. I'll go and rustle us up some pasta. Is that OK with you?"

"Fine. Are you sure I can't give you a hand?"

"No, I prefer to work on my own in the kitchen. Frank always got under my feet, so I refuse to have anyone else in there whilst I'm cooking!"

"OK then, I know my place. I'll go and see what's on the box."

*

"That was amazing, Liz, thank you. I can't remember the last meal I didn't cook. I could get used to this!" As soon as he had uttered the words, Tom regretted them. He had been careful all day not to say anything out of turn, but he need not have worried. Liz was happy to receive the compliment, and now that Tom was a free man, she didn't even mind the suggestion that they would see more of each other. The news of Brenda's passing saddened her, but at the same time, she couldn't help feeling that it made whatever she had with Tom more appropriate. Liz enjoyed his company and was happy at the thought of having it more often. After losing Frank, she could never have imagined that she would find another soulmate, but being reunited with Tom had circumvented all the awkwardness associated with dating. Although they had met after a lifetime apart, he still felt familiar. It was like putting on a very comfortable pair of slippers.

That night as Tom slipped between the covers next to Liz, he was overcome with emotion. Liz hugged his shaking body close to hers as she fought back her tears. Theirs was a heady mix of love, grief, regret, guilt, anticipation and solace. They were together now, and they could heal each other.

Liz was already up and dressed and in the kitchen making breakfast by the time Tom woke up. She was pleased he had stayed over, but she was also a seething mass of emotions. It was a lifetime since she had been intimate with anyone but Frank, and although she loved Tom, this new turn of events had caught her off guard.

Tom made an appearance an hour or so later. He had showered, and Liz couldn't deny how handsome he looked with his dewy-fresh skin and intoxicating smile. Frank had never been much of a morning person, and Liz had learned to keep out of his way until he had read the morning paper and dosed himself with several cups of strong coffee.

Tom looked altogether mellower. He breezed into the kitchen and greeted Liz with a kiss on her cheek before availing himself of the kettle. Liz liked how he was making himself at home, and she was pleased he felt relaxed in her domain.

"Should I give Christopher a ring and arrange for us to meet him so we can tell him about the money?"

"Yes, from what you were saying, he needs it as soon as possible. I can't stand the thought of him coming to any more harm. I still think we should tell the police, and it doesn't seem right that those thugs get all that money."

"I know what you mean, but if Christopher genuinely owes it to them, I am not sure we can intervene. I just hope they stick to their word and back off once he has paid his debt."

Chapter Thirty-Four

Brian wanted to talk. Of course, as soon as she had heard the words, she had agreed to him coming round. Was she too eager? Was she a pushover? She couldn't play games. If there was a chance that Brian wanted to go home, then she was prepared to listen to what he had to say. Yes, the last few weeks with Mike had been fun. He had made her feel like a woman again, not just a mother. She had enjoyed the attention and the sex, but she hated the infidelity. How could she judge Brian for having an affair when she had jumped into bed with another man at the drop of a hat? Did she somehow think that by her having an affair, they were now equal? This is not how she wanted to live her life. She was better than this. Then there were the boys to consider. They were the innocent victims in all this. They couldn't understand what they had done wrong to make their dad leave them. No amount of reassurance from Cheryl had convinced them that they were not to blame. She couldn't stand the thought of how much they were hurting. They would be so pleased to have their dad home. She owed it to them to at least try and reconcile things with Brian.

As Brian pulled into the driveway, he felt strangely nervous. This was his home and his wife. Why did he have butterflies? Perhaps it was because he felt like an absolute fool. It wasn't bad enough that he had screwed up his marriage by having an affair, but here he was just weeks after moving out, begging to be allowed back home. How could he have got things so wrong?

Even though he knew in his heart that being back with Cheryl and the boys was what he wanted, he still felt sick at abandoning Cath and the baby. He had meant it when he said he wanted to be part of the baby's life, but he had also meant it a few weeks ago when he left his marital home. Was he this shallow?

As he stepped across the threshold, Brian had the same feeling in his stomach as when they had gone to view the house for the first time as newlyweds. The hallway was airier than he remembered, the living room looked freshly painted, and the garden beyond the patio doors looked bigger.

He sat down in his favourite spot on the sofa, and Cheryl opted for the chair opposite. Then they began to talk. They talked about what had gone wrong and why. They talked about their feelings and their worries. They spoke of the boys and the new baby, the changes that would have to happen, and the needed compromises on both sides. They agreed that the counselling sessions were non-negotiable and that they had to find a way for some 'together time.' They talked about how to make it work with Cath and how Cheryl would let down Mike. They chatted as they had never done before, and then they hugged.

Chapter Thirty-Five

Four months later.

The supermarket trolley was so full Julie wondered if she would get all the groceries in her little car. She had probably overdone it but having suggested to everyone that she host a party for her dad's birthday, she felt obliged to put on a good show. Of course, once she had started selecting things to make a buffet, she had had to add in extra options for the children, and then there was the alcohol; by the time Julie got to the checkout, she was sincerely hoping that Brian would offer her something towards the cost of it all. Otherwise, she and Zane would be living off baked beans for the rest of the month.

They had all had such a turbulent time recently that her dad's birthday suddenly seemed the perfect excuse for a bit of fun. It had been a long time since they had all got together for a pleasant reason, instead of standing around a hospital bed or graveside and of course, this would be the first time that Christopher would experience a Beresford knees-up. When they were all in the right mood for a party, they knew how to have a good time. There would be plenty of food and drink, some silly party games to keep the children amused and then once the sun had dropped and the children had drifted off to bed, the grown-ups would sit out on the patio wrapped in blankets, warmed by the glow of the chiminea and swap stories into the early hours. She had fond memories of several such evenings. There would be one exceptional person missing from the celebration. Julie had wondered if that was reason enough not to suggest the party but having talked it over with Brian. Cheryl, they had all decided that Tom could do with a bit of fuss and hopefully, they could make it a lovely evening, and he wouldn't dwell on the fact that Brenda wasn't by his side.

They had also had to discuss the pros and cons of inviting Liz. Whilst it might have been an excellent way of everyone getting to know each other, they had decided that it was too soon, and it might feel as if Liz was somehow taking the place of Brenda. For now, they would keep the emphasis on Tom.

At 6 pm, the dining room table was groaning with an abundance of buffet favourites; there was even a trifle and a half-decent looking birthday cake that Julie had managed to whip up with Zane's help. Julie had turned the table around and pushed it up against the wall to create more space in her modest living room. Zane had gone to town blowing up balloons, and whilst it might have looked like they were ready to greet a hoard of six-year-olds, Julie couldn't help feeling she had done them proud. A few minutes later, she welcomed the first of her guests, Brian, Cheryl and the boys. Daniel and Archie were well impressed with the piles of sandwiches, sausage rolls and pork pie that greeted them and within minutes, the room filled with the raucous mix of music, laughter and childish giggles. By the time she opened the door to the guest of honour, the party was well underway.

"Thanks for this love ", beamed Tom handing Julie a bottle of red wine, "I think this is what we all needed. A chance to let our hair down."

"Happy birthday, dad. Come on in. Christopher is in the kitchen. He's just arrived and is getting a drink."

Christopher was in his element. He was accepted as part of the family by his father and half brother, and sister. When he had set out to trace his birth parents, he could never have imagined that things would have worked out so well. He couldn't think of many times in his life when he had felt happier. The only thing that would have improved this scene was if he could have shared it with his ex-wife and his daughter. More than anything, he regretted losing them.

He had been stupid and selfish. It was true what they say about not knowing what you have until it is gone. That was him. He was too busy getting rich to notice the harm he was doing at home.

Too keen to flash the cash with his mates down the pub to consider the impact he was having on his wife and young daughter. In the end, they had simply had enough of him. He was never there for them. He had never seen Amy in a school play or watched her trying her best at a sports day. He had stopped taking his beautiful wife out for dinner, stopped telling her she was beautiful. He would roll home in the early hours stinking of booze, and she would turn her back on him in disgust. Now he had a large designer home and a flash car on the drive, and nobody noticed.

"Grandad, this is for you,", said Zane handing Tom a misshapen present.

"Did you wrap this all by yourself?" Zane nodded proudly.

On opening the extravagantly wrapped gift, Tom was somewhat baffled to see a set of spark plugs. Not the usual thing for a five-year-old to present to their granddad, but Tom smiled in appreciation and made the appropriate cooing noises. Soon things became a little clearer as he unwrapped a socket set from Daniel and Archie and then a Haynes car manual for a 1964 Mini from Julie.

"There seems to be a bit of a theme forming here," he said after finally opening another weirdly shaped gift from Brian and Cheryl that contained a bucket and sponge. "I don't suppose any of this has anything to do with you, does it?" He shot a glance at Christopher.

"I don't know what you mean," he said, handing Tom a box that turned out to contain aftershave.

"Very droll," smiled Tom.

"Right, who wants cake," asked Julie.

Later, as predicted, the three boys settled in front

of the television to play one of Zane's computer games whilst the adults made the most of the late August warmth and drifted into the garden.

Tom looked the happiest anyone had seen him in months. Julie knew he was desperately missing Brenda, but she hoped the evening had given him a little pleasure. He must have read her mind.

Picking up his glass, he proposed a toast. "I just want to thank Julie for doing all this for me. It's been lovely to spend time with you all, and it's the first time we have laughed together in months. I appreciate it. Thanks, Julie. I want to welcome Christopher to the family and thank Brian and Julie for taking their long-lost brother to their hearts, and let's not forget those who are not with us tonight. Let's have a toast to mum; she always enjoyed a good party."

"To mum."

*

"Right young man, it's time for bed. Say goodnight to everyone."

"I want granddad to put me to bed, pleeease, mum," urged Zane.

"It's fine, Julie, I don't mind. Are Daniel and Archie staying here tonight?"

"No, dad, we'll have to get going ourselves soon. The boys are going to football practice tomorrow, part of half-term activities up at the school. Say goodnight to granddad and Zane boys. I'll call you in the week."

"OK, son, night boys, night Cheryl."

"Right, up to bed with granddad and no messing about. It's late now and time for bed."

"OK, mum. Night. Love you."

Zane ran up the stairs ahead of his granddad. Tom couldn't remember the last time he had got to put Zane to bed; it must have been at least six months ago. He rather enjoyed the bedtime routine, and he was sad that he had missed out on reading stories to Brian and Julie when they were little and breathing in their clean scent when they were fresh out of the bath.

As he tucked Zane into bed, he couldn't help feeling a pang of sadness for the little fellow. He had gone all his life without knowing what it was to have a father read him a bedtime story. Julie was a wonderful mum, and she had done a brilliant job at bringing him up single-handedly, but still, there was a definite father-shaped hole in Zane's life. Tom was so relieved that Brian had made up with Cheryl and always be there for Daniel and Archie. He had hated to think about the family breaking up and knew it had not been an easy decision for Brian. As it was, he was turning his back on the as yet unborn child, but Tom knew Brian would do all he could to be a father figure in that child's life as well.

"That was a good party Zane, don't you think so?"

"Yes. I liked the games, and Uncle Christopher is

cool."

"I'm pleased you like him. How many times have you met him, two?"

"No", Zane giggled, "more than that. He and mummy like to snuggle on the sofa, and one day we went to his house, and I saw them kissing."

Zane was now giggling uncontrollably and snorting into his pillow. He liked to tell tales, and he was rather pleased with this one.

Tom was not so pleased with the revelation. Was this true? Could Julie be carrying on with Christopher, her brother?

She didn't have a very good track record when it came to men. She had been on her own now for several months, as far as Tom knew. Had she taken advantage of Christopher coming into their lives? If she ended up falling out with him and driving him away, Tom wasn't sure he would be able to forgive her.

He rationalised in his spinning mind that they were not related by blood but still, the thought of his son and his daughter being anything more than platonic made his stomach churn.

Adopted or not, Tom had always considered Brian and Julie as his flesh and blood. As far as he was concerned, they were siblings. Christopher was no different. If he was Tom's son, he was Julie's brother, and brothers and sisters did not carry on with each other. He couldn't quite believe what he had heard. Leaving Zane, he made his way back downstairs, unsure what he might find. He needn't have worried. Christopher was sitting at the kitchen table, and Julie had her hands in the sink, washing out the wine glasses. He smiled at them.

No, it was all in Zane's imagination.

"Dad, can I have a quiet word with you?" Christopher asked. A warm glow enveloped Tom on hearing those words. How long he had waited to know the true meaning of the word 'dad. 'It was as remarkable now as all the times he had imagined hearing it in his first years of marriage. Whilst losing Brenda had torn his heart in two, having his biological child in his life had somehow made him complete again.

"I just wanted to say thank you again for helping me out. I haven't had any bother since I settled my debt, and I've been going to the GA sessions every week."

"That's great news. Liz will be pleased to hear it, and she has been worried sick about you."

"How's it going with Liz?"

"Rather well. We have seen rather a lot of each other, and I think Sarah is finally warming to the idea that her mother deserves to be happy again. You will have to come over to the house again before long, and we can all have a meal together."

"I'd like that."

The men were suddenly aware of a taxi pulling up outside the house.

"It is rather late to be having visitors. Are we expecting anyone else?"

A tall, dark-clothed figure emerged from the taxi and began to walk up the garden path, but Tom was none the wiser.

"Amy?" Christopher said incredulously. "What on earth are you doing here? How did you know where to come?"

Before she could answer, Christopher turned to Tom and whispered,

"Dad, meet your granddaughter."

This birthday just keeps getting better, thought Tom.

Printed in Great Britain
by Amazon